"I'M SORRY I CALLED YOU A SEWER RAT WHO LIVES IN a nest of horse manure."

He pulled his hand away from the silken softness of her face, hiding his sudden rush of emotion and need with a snort of laughter as he stood up. "No, you're not."

But she stood up, too, catching his hand in hers, bringing it up to the softness of her lips. She kissed his knuckles, and the featherlight sensation was totally unnerving.

"Yes, I am," she whispered. "I *am* sorry."

When she released his hand, he tried to convince himself that his sudden disappointment was in fact relief. But when she stepped even closer and reached up to touch the side of his face, he knew the truth. There was nothing in the world he wanted more than to kiss Marisala.

"We *are* friends," she said again. "When I'm with you, I can say what I want. And you—you can do the same, you know."

"I will," he whispered. He wanted to kiss her, but he'd never tell her that. He couldn't.

She pulled him close, not for a kiss, but to embrace him in a friendly hug.

He buried his face in the sweet-smelling mass of her beautiful hair. He could feel the softness of her breasts against his chest, feel her fingers lacing through his own hair, feel her thighs pressed against his as she stood on tiptoe.

And he was lost.

All he knew was that suddenly he was kissing her.

WHAT ARE *LOVESWEPT* ROMANCES?

They are stories of true romance and touching emotion. We believe those two very important ingredients are constants in our highly sensual and very believable stories in the LOVE-SWEPT line. Our goal is to give you, the reader, stories of consistently high quality that may sometimes make you laugh, sometimes make you cry, but are always fresh and creative and contain many delightful surprises within their pages.

Most romance fans read an enormous number of books. Those they truly love, they keep. Others may be traded with friends and soon forgotten. We hope that each LOVESWEPT romance will be a treasure—a "keeper." We will always try to publish

LOVE STORIES YOU'LL NEVER FORGET
BY AUTHORS YOU'LL ALWAYS REMEMBER

The Editors

Loveswept ® 873

FREEDOM'S PRICE

SUZANNE BROCKMANN

BANTAM BOOKS
NEW YORK · TORONTO · LONDON · SYDNEY · AUCKLAND

FREEDOM'S PRICE

A Bantam Book / January 1998

ISBN 0-553-44599-5

Published simultaneously in the United States and Canada

Bantam Books are published by Bantam Books, a division of Bantam Dou-
bleday Dell Publishing Group, Inc. Its trademark, consisting of the words
"Bantam Books" and the portrayal of a rooster, is Registered in U.S.
Patent and Trademark Office and in other countries. Marca Registrada.
Bantam Books, 1540 Broadway, New York, New York 10036.

PRINTED IN THE UNITED STATES OF AMERICA

OPM   10 9 8 7 6 5 4 3 2 1

To all of my fellow members
of Amnesty International,
who believe, as I do,
that writing a letter can
save a life, and that one voice,
when joined by thousands of others,
can make a difference

Acknowledgments

Special thanks to all of my new friends on the Internet—especially those from the RWL-List. Your support and help with research are hugely appreciated!

Dear Reader,

Marisala, the former freedom-fighting heroine in *Freedom's Price*, is a woman we can all relate to.

Like Marisala, we are forced in our busy lives to slip from role to role upon demand. True, not many of us are called upon to lead an army, but you'd better believe that if we had to, we certainly could.

Today's women are expected to hold down a high-powered job (the equivalent of being a warrior!), yet also be chief cook and housekeeper, Little League coach, gentle, feminine mommy, *and* somebody's steaming-hot lover.

We're also expected to know when to speak out and when to hold our tongues, which brings us back to Marisala, who—according to her uncle—needs a little help in that department!

Enter Liam Bartlett, assigned by her uncle—despite Marisala's protests—as her guardian. In the grand tradition of *Gigi*, Liam is called upon to teach Marisala how to behave less like a warrior and more like a woman.

She, however, has a thing or two to teach him. . . .

I hope you enjoy reading this story as much as I enjoyed writing it!

Suzanne Brockmann

ONE

"I'm sorry, we have no record of a Mary . . . Mara . . ."

"Marisala."

"We have absolutely no record of a Marisala Bolivar requesting student housing." The tired-looking woman behind the counter looked as if she were going to burst into tears. "Are you sure you sent in the required forms with your registration?"

"I'm sure of nothing," Marisala admitted, hiking her bag higher up on her shoulder. "My uncle handled all of the paperwork."

"Then it's possible we never received the forms." The administrator glanced toward the doors as they opened, then did a double take.

Marisala looked up to see Liam coming into the university housing office. Of course. She should have known. With his gleaming blond hair and his perpetual smile, Liam Bartlett was so handsome that whenever women—even tired women—saw him, they always looked twice.

She herself had done a double take when he'd surprised her by meeting her at Logan Airport.

"Believe it or not, I got a fabulous parking spot right out front," he told Marisala, oblivious to the fact that all of the women in the busy office had stopped to gaze at him. "Did you get your room assignment and your keys?"

"Not exactly."

He looked from Marisala to the housing administrator and back, his sunny smile fading. "Uh-oh," he said. "What happened?"

"Santiago messed up." Marisala knew she sounded a little too smug, but she couldn't help it. Although she liked being here in Boston, attending this university was all her uncle Santiago's idea. The courses of study he'd insisted she take seemed useless, and the fact that she was years older than the other students in the freshman class was embarrassing. Still, her uncle had made it clear she didn't have a choice in this matter. She was here to get educated, to become—in his words—civilized. "I think he forgot to send in the housing request."

Liam looked at the woman behind the counter. "I don't suppose you have a dorm room empty and waiting?"

For the first time since Liam had tapped her on the shoulder in the airport's baggage-claim area and she'd turned around to find herself gazing into his ocean-blue eyes, Marisala let herself really look at him.

He looked almost nothing like the frail, battered

man she'd helped escape from the war-torn island of San Salustiano five years earlier. Then he could barely walk, courtesy of the injuries he'd received in the war and the beatings he'd survived behind the hellish prison walls.

Now he was a picture of good health. While he was still lean, he was no longer skinny. His body was well muscled, filling out the softly faded blue jeans and the white shirt and sport jacket he wore.

He was—as the American magazines she'd read on the plane had defined it—a total babe.

On the other side of the counter, the housing administrator was shaking her head. "We have a wait list for campus housing that's already over a hundred names long." She looked at Marisala. "If you like, I can give you the forms you'll need to apply for university housing for the January semester."

Marisala leaned against the counter. "Sure. Why not?"

"Why not?" Liam didn't look happy. In fact, he was practically sputtering. "Why *not?* Because January's four months away—that's why not!" He turned back to the housing administrator. "Isn't there *some*thing you can do? She's a foreign student and—"

"No, I'm not." Marisala bristled in response. "I'm as much an American as you are." Her mother had been American. Marisala had dual citizenship.

Liam backpedaled. "What I meant was, it's not like your uncle lives fifteen minutes away in Newton."

"This is not that big a deal," she interrupted once again. "I'll find an apartment—"

"Oh, Santiago's going to *love* that."

Marisala couldn't hide her grin. "I know. Isn't that great?" She faced the housing administrator. "Can you give me a list of hotels in the area? Someplace I can stay temporarily?"

"Hotels?" Liam said. "Wait a minute—"

"I can give you a list," the woman said apologetically, "but I can also tell you that everything in this area is booked solid. Two conventions are in town, not to mention all the parents dropping students off at all the colleges and staying overnight. You might be able to find a motel room out in Natick or Framingham."

Marisala looked at Liam. "Do you know where Natick—"

"Yes, and it's too far away. How would you get to your classes?"

"It would be only temporary, until I can find—"

"An apartment, I know. You keep saying that, and I keep imagining Santiago coming after me with a gun."

Marisala laughed. "He wouldn't."

But Liam wasn't kidding. He stepped closer, lowering his voice to speak to her privately. Beneath the aroma of coffee and the light hint of expensive cologne, she could smell sunshine and laughter. She could smell that sweet, musky, unmistakably delicious and entirely male scent that was pure Liam Bartlett. And just like that, she was fifteen years old again and hopelessly in love with her uncle's Americano friend, the handsome young newspaper reporter with the sinfully sexy smile and exotic golden hair. "Mara, I promised him I'd look out for you."

She stepped back, trying to distance herself from the memory of old, long-faded feelings. She'd been so certain Liam would return to the tiny nation of San Salustiano after the civil war was finally over. She'd waited impatiently for him as days turned into weeks, weeks into months. It seemed impossible that he hadn't had an answering passion for her burning in his heart.

But she was wrong. Her grand passion had been tragically one-sided.

Now she kept her voice light. She was not the type to make the same mistake twice. She wouldn't misinterpret Liam's cheerful friendship as anything more than that again, no matter *how* good he smelled. "Good, you can fulfill your promise by helping me look for an apartment."

Liam ran his hands through his hair. He wore it much shorter now than he had all those years ago, and the new style suited him. His face had filled out too. It was broader, fuller and less boyish looking, although his smile was still pure ten-year-old. And even though he was no longer gaunt from hunger and mistreatment, his cheekbones still dominated his handsome face, highlighting his perfect nose, his elegantly shaped lips, and showcasing those incredible eyes.

His eyes hadn't changed at all. They were still the color of heaven on a sunny day.

"Mara, Santiago wanted you to live in a dormitory, not an apartment."

"Then he should have made sure he sent in the housing application." She couldn't hide her smile.

He frowned at her. "This isn't funny."

"Yes, it is. Come on, Liam, think about it. Santiago is always so perfect. This is one very large mistake for such a perfect man to make."

Liam looked at the girl standing in front of him. Woman, not girl. Despite the fact that she still looked and dressed like a fifteen-year-old, Marisala was twenty-two years old. She wasn't a child anymore.

"It's absurd, don't you think?" she added. "I've come all this way to find I have no place to live." Another smile played about the corners of her mouth. "It's about as absurd as the idea that I need a guardian to take care of me."

"*You* know you don't need a guardian, and *I* know you don't need a guardian." Liam kept his voice deceptively even, hiding the turmoil that had been swirling inside of him from the first moment he'd set eyes on her again at the airport. "But that's beside the point. Santiago asked me to do him this favor. How could I say no?"

"No." Her brown eyes were so dark, they seemed almost black as she gazed at him. "Just like that. Want me to show you how to do it again? *No*. It's really very easy."

When Liam looked into this girl's smiling eyes, he felt more alive than he had in years.

She was uncommonly beautiful, although someone walking past her on the street wouldn't stop and stare because she disguised it well. Her baggy clothes hid her perfect, trim body, and her thick mass of wavy brown hair was tied back in a sloppy ponytail at the nape of her neck. Her deceptively sweet heart-shaped face made her look younger than she was, as did her delicate nose and her sensuously full lips and elfishly pointed chin. She wore no makeup, and her skin was smooth and flawlessly clear, with the exception of a large crescent-shaped scar on her cheek, at the corner of her left eye— a grim reminder of the war she'd survived.

She hadn't just survived it, she'd fought and triumphed over it alongside men twice her size and weight. She'd taken charge in the chaos and smoke of battle and had become one of the guerrilla force's fiercest warriors, a tiny slip of a girl with the emotional strength of a giant.

But, with the exception of that scar, she didn't look much different than she had when they'd first met, back when she truly was only fifteen years old.

He'd been wildly attracted to her then too.

At the time he'd been smart enough and sane enough to recognize that his feelings were inappropriate. He was eight years her senior. He had been a grown man while she was just a kid. He'd locked everything he'd felt deep inside of him, forcing himself to ignore his attraction to Santiago's beautiful young niece, using his iron will to make himself forget he felt anything for her besides friendship.

And he *had* forgotten.

Until a few hours ago, when he'd picked her up at the airport.

When he'd seen her again, it had taken every ounce of strength in his body not to pull her into his arms and cover her mouth with his.

He *still* ached to kiss her.

But he couldn't. Not now. Not after his promise to Santiago. Like it or not, he had agreed to be Marisala Bolivar's temporary guardian.

"You have to tell Santiago you can't do this," Marisala told him.

God, he wished he could. He wished it were that easy. "I've already told him I would."

"Tell him you've changed your mind."

"Marisala, I promised him. Look, it's not really that big a deal." Liam tried to convince himself as well. He didn't dare tell her that Santiago had asked him to teach his willful niece how to behave less like the leader of a commando squad and more like a polite young lady during her stay here in Boston. He was going to give her time to adjust to being in a strange country before he told her that her uncle had asked him to school her in everything from how to dress, how to wear her hair, and most of all, how *not* to speak her mind with her usual frank bluntness at all times. "We'll have dinner once a week, touch base over the phone on the other days—"

"And I'll be required to report to you where I'm going, what I'm doing, and exactly who I'm doing it with." She rolled her eyes in exasperation. "He wouldn't treat me this way if I were a man."

"You're right," Liam agreed. "But old habits are hard to—"

"I spent nearly four years fighting to bring freedom to San Salustiano," Marisala interrupted gently. "I fought for freedom for all, not freedom for my uncle to tell me what I can and cannot do."

Liam glanced back at the woman waiting patiently

behind the counter. "We can argue politics some other time. Right now we have to figure out what I'm going to do with you."

It was a poor word choice. Her hackles rose visibly. "What *you're* going to do with me?" she repeated. "You don't have to *do* anything with me. In fact, you, my friend, can just go out to your car, take it from its *fabulous* parking space, and drive away. You can let *me* deal with *my* problem." She turned back to the counter, lifting her chin. "I'd like the names of those hotels in . . . wherever it was, please."

"Look, I've got a spare bedroom. I guess you can stay with me for a few days." Even before the words came out of his mouth, Liam knew saying them was a terrible mistake. It was going to be difficult enough seeing Marisala once or twice a week without wanting to touch her. Having her live with him in his house was sheer insanity.

But it was going to be only temporary.

"Gee," she said dryly, turning to gaze at him. "Don't sound so enthusiastic about it."

"It's just . . ." He started again. "It's not going to look good—you moving into my place, even for just a few days."

She lifted one eyebrow, gazing at him steadily. "We shared a one-room shelter in the jungle for nearly six months."

The had. And he'd spent half the time unconscious and weak from his injuries, and the other half of the time pretending that he felt nothing more than a brotherly affection for this girl. At the same time he'd been well aware of the speculation that had gone on. He'd overheard the gossip that he and Marisala were lovers. When he'd found out about the untrue assumptions, he'd been ready to sleep outside of the tent—until Marisala had bluntly informed him that the rumors that she was "the Americano's" woman kept away unwanted male attention.

"I don't want Santiago to think—"

"Santiago's biggest wish is for me to be distracted by a lover who will keep me smiling and get me pregnant, whereupon I'll have to marry and then will be forever out of my uncle's hair." Her gaze turned speculative. "I wouldn't put it past Santiago to have sent me to Boston in hopes that you would give me a whole hell of a lot more than your protection as my 'guardian,' if you know what I mean."

Liam knew exactly what she meant. And although Santiago had definitely wanted Liam to be much more than Marisala's guardian, becoming her lover *wasn't* what the older man had in mind.

"In fact," Marisala continued, a sparkle of amusement in her eyes as she leaned closer and lowered her voice, "I can just picture Santiago sending his assistant, Raphael, up here to Boston with an order to sneak into your home and stick pinholes into the tips of all of your condoms."

"Marisala!" Liam felt his face heat with a blush, and he turned away, hoping she wouldn't see how her frankness had unnerved him. He turned to implore the housing administrator, "Please. Are you absolutely positive there's nothing you can do to help?"

The woman had returned to sorting through files, and now she looked up distractedly. "We're opening the gym for students who have housing problems. If she has a sleeping bag, your girlfriend is welcome to stay there for a few nights until other arrangements can be made."

"She's not my girlfriend," Liam protested.

Marisala took a step back in surprise at his vehemence. He'd certainly been quick to make sure everyone in the room knew that they weren't lovers. She tried not to care. Why should she care? "I'm his ward," she added.

Liam snorted. "Come on, you are not. Not really."

She gazed at him. "Then what would you call it?"

"I don't know. But not *ward*. That sounds so archaic."

"That's because it *is* archaic." Marisala turned to the housing administrator. "How many twenty-two-year-old women do *you* know who have a guardian?"

The housing administrator blinked. "Well, I know quite a few of our foreign students have sponsors or mentors—"

"Mentor." Liam snapped his fingers. "That's what you can call me."

"No." Marisala shook her head. "I'm almost positive my uncle had something more dominant and submissive in mind."

She was playing with him, seeing if her words would make him blush again. She hadn't realized he was such a . . . She searched for the English word. A *prude*. He hadn't seemed to care much about what anyone thought of their living arrangement back in the jungles of San

Salustiano. But maybe it was different here. After all, Boston was a different world from her island homeland. Here he had friends and coworkers living nearby.

Maybe Liam had a lover, a lady friend who wouldn't approve of or appreciate Marisala's temporary stay, even if it were only in his spare bedroom.

She glanced up at him to see if that was the reason behind his reluctance to share his home with her, and the flare of sudden heat in his eyes caught her off guard.

"Dominant and submissive," he repeated. "You mean, something more like master and slave?" His voice was soft but intense, and the look in his eyes was pure male. It was not a look she had ever seen before—at least not in *his* eyes. "Don't push too hard, *cara*," he murmured, "or you might get more than you bargained for. I may be your guardian, but I'm only human."

This time *she* was the one with the pink tinge of a blush decorating her cheeks. She tried to hide her sudden confusion with a joke. "Perhaps we should call you my 'wrangler.' You know, kind of like the men who are in charge of making the wild animals behave on a movie set?"

Liam laughed at that, but the intensity lingered in his eyes. "Come on, wild thing, let's get out of here. I've got a meeting in less than an hour. I have just enough time to drop you off at home."

Marisala thanked the woman behind the counter before following Liam back out to his car.

The sunlight was hazy, the late afternoon was thick with humidity, and Liam's words seemed to hang in the air around her. *Don't push too hard*, cara, *or you might get more than you bargained for*.

Marisala got into the car, hardly daring to glance at the man sitting beside her.

Mother of God, was it possible that Liam Bartlett was actually attracted to her too?

He started the engine with a roar. She watched his long fingers gently maneuver the stickshift into first gear, and for the first time in years she allowed herself to imagine him touching her with those elegant hands. Kissing her. She'd imagined him kissing her so many times before.

He would be so gentle. His lips would be so soft as his mouth brushed against hers. He'd pause, pulling back to gaze at her, the ocean blueness of his eyes so warm as he smiled. And then he'd kiss her again, gently and so sweetly, almost worshipfully parting her lips with his tongue.

Marisala knew it by heart. It was a fantasy that had sustained her through the darkness of night on more than one occasion. Yet now, for the first time in years, she was actually daring to believe it could come true.

Because maybe, just maybe, Liam found her attractive too.

Marisala gazed out at the unfamiliar city streets, remembering that unmistakable heat she'd seen in his eyes. It had frightened and even shocked her a little bit. And it had excited her too. He was human, he'd said. Don't push him. She realized that during all those years she'd daydreamed of him, she'd dreamed about someone perfect, someone not quite human.

In her dreams he'd undressed her slowly, carefully, his eyes not hot with desire but warm with love. He'd touched her, kissed her, he'd taken his slow, sweet, gentle time to love her completely.

But maybe her dreams had been wrong. Maybe if she kissed him, that hot fire she'd seen burning in his eyes would take control. Maybe his passion would explode, sending her to a place she'd never been before.

She would surrender herself to him, giving him what she'd given no man—a glimpse of her heart and soul.

But just a small glimpse, because she was no longer a wide-eyed innocent schoolgirl. She was old enough now to know quite well the difference between love and lust. And her dreams no longer ended with promises of forever.

She no longer wanted them to end that way.

A moment of shared passion was all she desired now. A temporary joining of bodies, accompanied by a brief touching of souls, with a borrowed feeling of completeness.

She could give him no more than that.

But that was all right, because he wouldn't want anything more.

If he'd wanted more, he would have come back to San Salustiano. He would have found her again, years ago.

"I'm not going to have time to do more than unlock the door and let you in. You can put your stuff in any of the extra bedrooms." Liam's voice broke into her thoughts. He glanced up from the road to smile at her.

"You'll have no problem figuring out which room is which. Mine's the one that's a mess."

"Ah," she said, working hard to keep her own voice light. "I guess some things never change."

"If you're hungry, help yourself to whatever you can find in the kitchen. It's all up for grabs. My meeting shouldn't go more than a half an hour. I'll pick up a pizza and a paper on the way home. We can check the classified ads and see about finding you an apartment."

"Where's your meeting?" she asked as he turned onto a street that was lined with well-kept and charming old town houses and apartment buildings.

"Over at the *Globe*. That's the newspaper office," he explained.

Marisala gave him a disgusted look. "I *know* what the *Globe* is. I read your column all the time, you know."

"I didn't know. Hey, look at this—a spot right in front of my building. You must be some kind of good-luck charm." A car parked along the street was pulling out, and Liam waited, signaling for the parking spot.

"Santiago has a copy of *The Boston Globe* sent to his office every week," Marisala told him, looking up at the building that Liam called home. It was six stories high and made of beautiful stone. "He always passed it on to me."

The parking space seemed only a few inches larger than Liam's car, yet he zipped into it quickly and efficiently as he focused most of his attention on her. "Really? Every week?"

"Every week for the past two years. It's the first thing I look at when I open the paper."

"I'm honored."

"You wrote some very powerful articles. Although lately—"

"Hey, did you get a chance to see the CNN report? You know, that piece I did on—"

"San Salustiano," she finished for him. "Of course. You know, if you'd written it for *The New York Times*, you might have won a Pulitzer."

"I chose CNN because my goal was for more everyday, average people to be aware of the problem—not to win awards." The U.S. government had been sending weapons and financial aid to the so-called democracy that used terror and military force to rule San Salustiano. Liam's series of news reports on the Cable News Network had brought forth a public outcry, and U.S. aid had stopped. Without that assistance, the people of the small island nation had quickly taken control of their government, democracy had been restored, and the war ended. A fair election had been held, and true leaders of the people—including Marisala's uncle—had been voted into office.

The island still had many problems, but at least fear of death or torture at the hands of the secret police wasn't among them.

"Besides," Liam added, smiling at her as he pulled up the parking brake and turned off the engine, "I *did* win an Emmy."

"And I know you'd *much* rather have an Emmy than a Pulitzer." Marisala smiled, amusement dancing in her eyes.

Liam couldn't keep from smiling back at her, but

still, this was far too serious a topic for him to make jokes. "I wanted for the war to end, *cara,*" he said quietly. "I wanted only to know that you were safe."

Her eyes widened and her lips parted slightly as she gazed at him, and he realized how intimate his words must have sounded. *Cara.* Liam had never called Marisala that before. But somehow today the term of endearment was slipping out whenever he turned around.

"I wanted to know that you and your uncle were safe," he quickly amended. "You and Diego and Juan and Garcia and Carmelita and everyone else who fought to keep their families together."

She glanced away from him then, her long eyelashes thick and dark against her cheeks.

Liam got out of the car, afraid if he sat there much longer, he'd do something utterly foolish like reach out and touch her hair. Or pull her into his arms and kiss her.

God, what a mess *that* would make. Even if he reached for her and she went willingly into his arms instead of throwing him over her shoulder and down onto the ground in some kind of hand-to-hand combat move, he couldn't ignore the fact that he'd made a promise to her uncle.

Despite the fact that she didn't need one, he was Marisala's guardian. He was supposed to take care of her, not take her to bed.

"Nice neighborhood," she said as she climbed out of his car. She stretched as she looked around, lifting both arms over her head and reaching for the sky.

She was wearing a plain white T-shirt, softened and shrunken from too many washings. It clung to her narrow shoulders yet gave only the merest suggestion of the slight feminine curves of her breasts.

She may have been seven years older, but she was still built like a fifteen-year-old, with smoothly tanned arms that were thin but strong.

She wore a pair of army fatigues that were a bit too big for her slender frame. They slid down on her hips, creating a gap between the waistband of her pants and the edge of her T-shirt, exposing a fraction of an inch of the soft smoothness of her stomach and revealing enticing glimpses of her belly button.

"I bought a condo here after my book made the *Times* list." Liam tried not to look at her, tried to focus on taking her suitcase out of the back of his car. But as he straightened up and shut the car door, she took it from him, her hand slipping underneath his on the handle. She seemed thoroughly unaware that she'd touched him, unaware that her touch had sent a jolt of electricity screaming through him.

"That's right. I'd almost forgotten. I'm in the company of a celebrity." She smiled at him. "A famous author with a book still on the best-seller list."

"It's not *still* on the list," he corrected her. "The paperback's just come out, and now it's on *that* list."

He was fascinated by the sight of her collarbone, exposed by the time-relaxed crewneck of her T-shirt. Those delicate bones seemed so fragile and feminine and out of place with the tough-as-nails image she exuded.

God help him, he was in trouble here. He was completely and thoroughly tuned in to this girl. He was aware of her every move, her every breath. He was in serious danger of being hypnotized simply from looking into her eyes. Still, he couldn't look away.

"So here's a question you probably get all the time," she continued, smiling up at him. "When's the next book coming out?"

Now Liam could look away. He had to. Because he couldn't look her in the eye and lie. If he did, she'd see right through him. He pretended to search through his keys as he led the way up to the front door of his building.

At one time he would have told her the truth. Back in San Salustiano, he'd been honest with her about everything—except for his inappropriate attraction to her. But it had been so long since he'd allowed himself that kind of openness, he gave her the same stock answer about his next book that he gave everyone who asked. "I'm working on it."

The truth was, he *wasn't* working on it. He was dodging his New York editor's weekly phone calls. He was doing everything and anything besides sitting down and writing that damned book.

He pointedly changed the subject. "There's a doorman who comes on duty at night," he said as he held the door open for her. "I'll introduce you to him later."

"Santiago told me this next book is a personal account of your experiences in San Salustiano." Marisala was watching him closely, her eyes searching his face. Several wild tendrils of dark hair had escaped from her ponytail, and the bright afternoon sun gave them golden highlights.

"Yeah." He reached for her suitcase as he opened the door that led to the stairs. "Let me take your suitcase. I'm up in the penthouse—the sixth floor."

"Doesn't the elevator work?"

"Yeah, but I'd rather take the stairs. I . . . I could use the exercise." Another lie.

Marisala was quiet as they started up the stairs.

Liam felt the need to fill in the silence. "Maybe after dinner we can go out and I'll show you around the university campus. We can look at your schedule and find where you'll be having your classes."

She spoke then. "Liam, I don't need a baby-sitter. I know you've got things you need to do—"

"Yeah, I've got things to do, but getting you settled is on the top of the list." Liam slowed his pace as they climbed upward, aware that Marisala was lagging slightly behind. No doubt she was tired from her long plane flight. And, unlike him, she wasn't used to jogging up and down six flights of stairs three or four times a day.

"What exactly did Santiago ask of you?"

"I told you. Dinner a couple times a week."

"Aha. A *couple* times. First it was *once* a week. Now the truth comes out. What else?"

"Like I said, we talk on the phone. No biggie."

"Uh-huh. What else?"

God, he'd forgotten how like a pit bull Marisala could be. Once she grabbed onto something, she wouldn't let go.

She was going to have a cow when she found out that her uncle had asked Liam to teach her to behave like a "civilized" young woman. He knew he was going to have to tell her sooner or later, but right now he chose later.

"He asked me to show you around Boston, around the university. He asked me to help you find your classes and your nonexistent dorm," Liam listed on his fingers. "Let's see, he asked me to help you find a doctor. He asked me to be available, particularly during these first few weeks, in case you need me."

Marisala was scowling. "He thinks I'm a child." Her eyes were blazing as she glowered up at Liam. "I'm *not* a child."

"Hey, I'm not the bad guy here."

Marisala snorted. "No, you're merely his accomplice."

"Mara, if you stop to think about it, you'll realize that Santiago's only crime is loving you too much."

"Too much of *any*thing can kill you."

Liam shook his head. "Not too much love. There's no such thing as too much love." They'd reached the top floor, and stood now, outside of his condo door.

Marisala gazed up at him, her dark eyes so serious. But then she smiled, her face softening. "Yeah, I guess you're right." She sighed. "But sometimes it can be pretty damn stifling."

Liam unlocked his door. "Maybe." But sometimes it could be lifesaving. He stepped back to let her go inside. "Make yourself at home, all right? I'll be back in an hour or so."

She paused just inside the door. "Liam, why does Santiago want you to help me find a doctor? I'm not sick."

He chose his words carefully, trying not to offend her. "He thought that while you were in Boston you should see a plastic surgeon, you know, to see if there was anything that could be done to make the scar on your face less noticeable."

But he should have known better. She wasn't offended. In fact, she laughed. "I *like* my scar," she countered, lifting her chin proudly. "It's part of who I am. It lets the world know where I've been and what I've done."

"I think Santiago's just trying to help."

"If he *truly* wants to help, he would let me live my own life."

"It's hard for him to—"

"It's hard for *me!* Do you *know* what he did—" She caught herself. "I'm sorry. You have to go."

Liam nodded. "We'll talk later, okay?"

Marisala nodded too. Her smile was rueful. "We'll talk later. And later. And later again. We're going to talk until we're blue in the face—the way we used to do, staying up long past midnight. And you are *so* going to regret getting involved with Santiago and me again."

Liam shook his head. "No, I won't."

She rolled her eyes. "Yes, you will. Just wait."

TWO

"I don't get it." Lauren Stuart, Liam's editor at *The Boston Globe*, leaned back behind her desk and gave him a long appraising look. "I thought you were excited about writing that piece about the statewide sex-offender registry that's gone into effect."

"I was." He resisted the urge to stand and pace back and forth across the room. He knew exactly why he couldn't sit still, why he'd turned into a pressure cooker about to explode. It had nothing to do with impending work deadlines and everything to do with the fact that right now, right this very moment, Marisala Bolivar was in his condo, waiting for him to come home.

He couldn't wait to get back there for another dose of the rollercoaster effect he felt from looking into her midnight-brown eyes.

Yet at the same time he dreaded going home. He knew damn well he wasn't going to sleep at all tonight. He was going to lie in bed, staring up at the dark ceiling, while every single cell in his body hummed with the knowledge that he and Marisala were alone in his apartment.

"I was," he repeated, trying to bring himself back to here and now. It was going to be tough enough to live through tonight. There was no need to experience that torture an extra time in anticipation. "But there's no way I'm going to get it finished by the deadline. Something's come up—a personal obligation that I've got to take care of."

"I see." Lauren nodded her perfectly coiffed blonde head. "All right. We'll reprint something you wrote a few years ago."

Liam looked over at her in surprise. "That's it? Just all right? No questions? No third degree? No Spanish Inquisition?"

"Would it put that article on my desk in time?" she asked, then answered her own question. "No. Would it help? No, not unless my goal was to get you wound even *tighter* than the high-pitched violin string you resemble." She reached forward and toppled the brass nameplate on her desk, revealing another sign that read THE EDITOR IS OUT. "Off the record, Lee, friend to friend, I wish you would—"

"I'll have something for you next week. I promise."

"Something," she repeated, lifting one elegant eyebrow.

He had to look away. "Yeah. I don't know if I'll have enough time to do the research for—"

"Stop," she said. "Just stop."

Liam looked up at her then. She didn't look happy.

As he watched she stood and moved to shut her office door. He caught an enticing whiff of her delicate and extremely expensive trademark perfume and heard the soft whisper of silk as she moved past him. As usual, Lauren Stuart was impeccably dressed in an elegant designer suit. She was wearing her jacket despite the heat of the late-summer day and still managed to look as cool and crisp as ever.

There was no doubt about it. Beautiful, sophisticated, elegant, and intelligent, with a body to die for and a brain and quick wit that was sharp as a sword, Lauren Stuart was a knockout. They'd been fast friends from the first moment they'd met, after his San Salustiano reports had aired on CNN.

Liam had been presumed dead for more than two years, falsely listed among the casualties in the deadly bombing of a civilian bus that occurred outside of the capital city of Puerto Norte in San Salustiano. His staff position at the *Globe* had long since been filled when he returned, but Lauren had quickly made room for him, giving him the cushy job of Sunday columnist, then offering him a chance to syndicate his extremely popular issues-oriented articles in other papers across the country.

There had once been a time when Liam would have pursued Lauren simply because she was bright and beautiful. He would have attempted to get her into bed as a matter of course. And odds were he would have succeeded.

But he'd come back from the hell he'd endured on San Salustiano with an ability to see beyond the instant gratification he'd always gone after in the past. And when he'd looked at Lauren, he got a clear glimpse of their two possible futures. One involved a love affair gone far too quickly stale because neither of their hearts would have been in it. The other was based instead on a strong and healthy platonic friendship.

He'd chosen friendship, and he'd never regretted it once.

"What's the deal, Lee?" Lauren asked quietly as she sat back behind her desk. "I thought you were jazzed about investigating the strengths and weaknesses of the sex-offender registry."

He gestured to the sign on her desk. "I thought the editor was out."

She leaned forward, impaling him with the no-nonsense crystal blueness of her eyes. "I'm asking you this as your *friend*, cowboy. I thought you told me this story was going to be the one to pull you out of your slump."

"Yeah, well, it's not." He rubbed his eyes, applying pressure to what was promising to be one hell of a head-ache.

Lauren was silent for a solid thirty seconds. It had to be some kind of a record for her.

"So it's finally happened, hasn't it?" she finally said. "You're thoroughly, totally, absolutely blocked."

He looked up. "No! I said, I have this obligation and—"

The language she used was extraordinarily pungent. "You couldn't write this piece on the registry to save your life."

"I sure as hell could—"

"Then do it," she challenged him. "Four years ago you could write an award-winning article on any compelling social issue in twenty minutes. Less. Today, you're taking two and a half weeks and coming up with articles about . . . what was last week's gem? Little stuffed animal toys called Beanie Babies?"

"It's an outrageous phenomenon," Liam said defensively. "Every kid in America has half a dozen of 'em."

"And you believe this information rates right up there with your reports on that Boston soup kitchen that lost its funding, or on the possibility of reinstating the death penalty in Massachusetts? Or how about that little exposé you did on that local right-to-life group that openly condoned violence, even murder, as a means to stop abortion? Oh, and then there was that piece you did on the resurgence of heroin as a recreational drug? Heroin. Beanie Babies. Sure, I can see the similarities."

"You're a real stand-up comic today. A barrel of laughs."

"I'm not laughing. And you're not either. As a matter of fact, you haven't laughed out loud in at least a year. Longer."

It was true. Everything she was saying was absolutely true. The depression that had caught hold of him upon his return home from San Salustiano had sunk its teeth into him again. He couldn't deny it. He couldn't explain it. But he could try to sidestep it. "I need some aspirin."

"I have everything *but* aspirin." Lauren reached into her desk drawer and took out four bottles of different over-the-counter pain remedies and lined them up on the edge of her desk. "Take your pick. But I doubt it's what you really need."

She opened the compact refrigerator that was positioned within reach of her chair and pulled out two bottles of sparkling water. She set one on her desk and handed the other to Liam.

"Thanks." He took the nearest plastic container of painkiller and popped the top open, dashing two colorful little pills into the palm of his hand. "I should get going." He couldn't bring himself to meet her eyes.

"What, without telling me about this annoying obligation that's suddenly sprung up out of nowhere?"

"It's—*she's* not annoying. And I thought you weren't interested."

"Aha. It's a she." Lauren opened her own bottle of water and poured it into an elegantly shaped glass. "Now I *am* interested. Especially since you haven't been interested in much of anything—female or otherwise— since last summer. What was the name of that last obligation? Janice? . . ."

"Janessa." Liam shook his head. "And she wasn't an obligation. She was . . ." He closed his eyes briefly. "I don't know what she was. A mistake, I guess." He tossed the pills into his mouth and washed them down with the bubbling water, drinking directly from his bottle. "Still, this obligation isn't what you think."

"What I *thought* was that you might've been working on an article about celibacy in this age of STDs, but since it's been nearly a full calendar year since Janessa took her sweet little pout and walked out of your life, I've changed my mind. I seriously doubt you're researching the lifestyle of a Franciscan monk." Lauren narrowed her eyes. "However, it's occurred to me that whatever's bugging you, getting laid sure couldn't make it any worse. So maybe you should stop and buy a nice bottle of wine on your way to meet that new little obligation and—"

"Stuart! God! My obligation happens to be Santiago Bolivar's niece!"

"Bolivar. Bolivar . . . Isn't that the name of your friend in San Salustiano?"

Liam jiggled his foot in a burst of nervous energy. "Yeah."

"And the niece . . . Wait—what was her name?"

"Marisala." God, he couldn't even say her name without feeling a flash of heat.

"She was the one who helped your brother and his wife get you off the island."

"Yeah."

"The teenager. The seventeen-year-old guerrilla Amazon."

"She's not an Amazon. She's a tiny little . . . girl."

"I was speaking figuratively. Amazon as in female warrior."

Liam couldn't sit still any longer. He got to his feet and started to pace. "Santiago's sending her to college here in Boston. He's asked me to give her any help she needs. And she does need help. There's been a mix-up with the campus housing, and I'm going to have to help her find an apartment near mine."

"An apartment in the Back Bay in September?" Lauren laughed. "Good luck."

"Thanks, Stuart. Your encouragement is greatly appreciated."

"So where's she staying until . . ." Lauren laughed again. "Oh, my. She's staying at your place, isn't she?"

"Yeah."

"Oh, Lee, don't fight it. This girl could be exactly what you n—"

"No. No way."

"What is that they always say about protesting too much? . . ."

Liam turned toward the door. "Look, I have to go—"

"Maybe, at the very least, you can *talk* to her."

"I'll give you a call over the next few days."

Lauren stood up. "She was there, too, Lee. . . ."

"In the meantime I'll work on that article and—"

" . . . and you've got to talk to someone!"

He stopped then, turning to look back at her. "There's nothing to talk about."

"Obviously. Especially since you've never so much as *mentioned* what happened to you in that San Salustiano prison. You know, at first I thought you weren't talking about it because you were writing a book about your experiences. But it's been five years and there's been no book."

"I started one. I couldn't . . ." Liam shook his head. "I couldn't do it." Writing down what he'd been through had been too painful. It was easier to lock his hellish experience deep inside of him and just try to go on with his life, pretending it never happened.

"All I know is that you went down there to report on

the political situation and the government stuck you in some prison and told your family you were dead."

Liam stared across the room at his friend. He'd always been grateful that Lauren had never asked about his experience in San Salustiano before. And she still wasn't asking him to tell her about it now. He knew she'd never do that, but she *was* giving him a clear invitation to volunteer the information.

With a sigh, he sat back down. Lauren Stuart was his friend. She deserved to know at least the basic facts. But that was all he could tell her. He'd told no one more than that. Even his good friend Kayla, his brother Cal's wife, had heard only an extremely edited version of the horrors he'd endured in that hellhole of a prison.

"I went to San Salustiano seven years ago, to meet with Santiago Bolivar," Liam recited. It helped to tell this story as if it had happened to someone else and not to him. "At the time Santiago had run for president against the incumbent, and lost despite a large showing of public support. He was convinced the results had been tampered with, and that the entire election had been a sham. When I went down to talk to him, little pockets of violence and resistance to the special police force had already sprung up, all over the island."

He paused, remembering that evening he'd spent, sharing dinner with Santiago Bolivar and his family. Marisala had been there, sitting quietly in the background as the men had talked about the possibility of an all-out war, of a political coup to regain control of their beloved country. And when Liam had finally gone out to his battered rental car, to head back to the hotel in the city of Puerto Norte, she had followed him.

"I met Marisala that first night," he told Lauren, trying to keep his voice devoid of emotion. But he couldn't. Where Marisala was concerned, he simply couldn't help himself at all. "She was fifteen years old, and . . ."

So beautiful. So young and innocent and pure. He could still see her coming out of the shadows beside Santiago's house to introduce herself. She'd had something to say to the Americano, and despite the fact that she was a mere girl, she was determined to say it.

"She begged me to talk sense into the men," he continued, "to keep them from turning this political disagreement into a war. We talked for a long time—she knew a little English, and I knew a bit of Spanish, and I swear, Stu, I'd never met anyone like her before, but she was just a *child*. Anyway, she told me she was afraid for her uncle's safety.

"And rightly so," he added, feeling the familiar queasiness in his stomach. He tried to step back, to push his feelings aside. He was a journalist. It helped if he remembered that—if he focused on the facts alone. "Two days later I met Santiago at a Puerto Norte café, and somehow the special police found out about it. They came to arrest us both. I knew as soon as they realized I was an American reporter, they'd make me disappear—probably permanently—so I ran."

He couldn't look at Lauren, couldn't look anywhere but out the window at the skyline of Boston. He didn't want to think about the force of that bullet that had hit him in the back, throwing him forward and down into the dirt.

"I got away, but I was badly wounded. I knew I couldn't make it off the island the conventional way because the police were looking for me. I didn't know where else to turn, so I went to Marisala. She hid me."

Lauren nodded. "Go on."

"I was hurt pretty bad, and it was about six months before I could even walk again—before I was even strong enough to survive the boat ride that would take me off San Salustiano." Liam massaged his temples.

"What happened to Santiago?"

"He was in prison all that time. But we didn't even know if he was still alive."

"This wasn't when your brother went down there looking for you, was it?"

Liam shook his head. "No. This was more than a year before that. The special police found out about the boat Marisala's father had rented, and figured correctly that it was for me, since I was still at large. The government wanted to make damn sure that I didn't get off the island. I knew too much. So they searched the entire village, and when they couldn't find me, Tomás Vásquez, the captain of the special police, threatened to burn it. He threatened to kill all of the men and boys if I didn't come forward."

He tried to make his voice more matter-of-fact, tried to feel as detached as he sounded, tried to report only the facts. But the facts were brutal and his voice cracked. "So I turned myself in, but Vásquez burned the village and killed the men and boys anyway. Marisala's father and brother were among the murdered."

Lauren drew in a breath, and Liam tried to fight the memories. He'd been there. He'd watched as that monster had given the order to gun down those innocent people. Marisala had been there too. He couldn't help but remember the sheer horror in her eyes. He couldn't erase the image of her fighting to free herself from the other women who held her, fighting to run to her father and brother, even though they were already dead, even though she herself would then be in range of those deadly machine guns.

"That's when Marisala joined the guerrilla forces. I went to prison," he stated, "and Marisala took up her father's gun and went to war."

It was amazing. With a few sentences, Liam could simplify and describe eighteen months of sheer hell.

"Since Marisala was Santiago's niece, it didn't take her long to win the respect and following she needed to become a leader in the rebel movement. By the time she was seventeen, she was making command decisions and leading from the front lines."

"Isn't that unusual?" Lauren asked, uncrossing and recrossing her legs with another whisper of silk. "Aren't women considered second-class citizens in that country?"

Liam nodded. "Yeah. It was unusual. *She's* unusual."

"That's obvious."

"Eventually, the rebel army attacked the prison where I was being held, and I was freed. Sort of. Everyone and their brother, including Tomás Vásquez himself, was after me. And after all those months in prison, I wasn't in real good shape."

Another massive understatement.

"That was when my brother and his wife came to the island," Liam continued. "And with their help, Marisala got me to safety."

Lauren took a delicate sip from her glass of water. "So now this Marisala is in Boston."

"She's a freshman at the university, but someone screwed up, and she doesn't have a dorm room."

"So she's staying with you."

"Only for a few nights." Please God, let them find a safe, clean apartment first thing in the morning.

"Lee, I hate to suddenly turn editor on you, but do you think Marisala would consent to an interview for the paper? This story is incredible and—"

"No." He glared at her. "Absolutely not. No way. Santiago made me her guardian, and *I* won't consent. She doesn't need to be reminded of that hell all over again. And God knows she doesn't need the notoriety. Santiago wants her to have a normal, quiet, *civilized* life now."

Lauren took another sip of her sparkling water, gazing at him over the top of the glass. "Maybe so. But what does *Marisala* want?"

Marisala wanted to go into Liam's room.

She'd been standing in the doorway for several long minutes, trying to decide whether Liam's casual "make yourself at home" included exploring his bedchamber.

Across the room, his bed was an unmade jumble of brightly patterned sheets and pillows. It was bigger than a normal double bed, perfect for two lovers to sleep comfortably—stretched out yet still touching, replete after making deliciously passionate, pulse-pounding love.

Against the other wall was a dresser, its wood stain a deep, rich brown. And several exercise machines were set up and ready for use in front of the windows.

The curtains were still closed, keeping all but a single red-orange ray from the setting sun out of the room.

Make yourself at home.

Marisala knew quite well that Liam hadn't meant for her to go into his bedroom and lie down on his bed, but she didn't care. She did it anyway. His sheets smelled like him and she lay back against his pillows, breathing in his masculine scent.

His bedroom looked even nicer from this angle.

There was a small clock radio sitting on an elegantly simple bedside table, and Marisala reached for it, switching it on.

She'd been looking for a radio for the entire hour that Liam had been gone.

His condo was much too quiet.

There was a complicated home electronics system down in Liam's enormous living room, but the only thing she'd managed to turn on was the television. But TV bored her. She'd wanted music to help fill the empty rooms of this ridiculously huge condominium that Liam called home. How many rooms did one man need? Liam had eight, not counting the three bathrooms. Three! What a decadent, luxurious, incredible waste of space for a man living alone.

And he did live alone. There was nothing in any of the other rooms that even remotely suggested that another person—that a woman—lived with him.

As the sound of jazz filled the room Marisala turned the radio's dial, searching for a Spanish station. She found a familiar merengue beat and lay back against the pillows.

Yes, she liked this room.

She would like it even better if Liam were here, in this bed with her.

He wanted her. He wanted *her*. The thought still made her want to laugh aloud. But she knew it was true. She'd seen it in his eyes.

She wasn't in love with him. Not anymore. Too much had happened. Too many years had passed.

But wanting and loving weren't even close to being the same thing. And love was far too complicated and binding, anyway. But the heat of desire was an entirely different matter.

Especially since Liam Bartlett was the sexiest man she'd ever known. He was quite possibly the sexiest man in the entire world.

And Marisala was here, living with him in his house until she found her own apartment.

With any luck, it wouldn't be that easy to find an apartment. With any luck, she'd have to stay here for days. Weeks, even.

And sooner or later the fire she'd seen in Liam's eyes would consume them both.

Sooner. She hoped it would be sooner.

Restlessly, she stood up and prowled around the room. The blue carpet under her bare feet was impossibly soft and thick. The dark-stained wood of his dresser was as smooth as satin beneath her fingers.

She gazed at the pictures scattered across the dressertop, picking up a wedding portrait. The groom was Liam's brother, Cal. Half brother, she remembered. Cal was dark-haired, dark-complexioned, and intensely serious, as different from Liam as he could possibly be, with the exception of his rather startlingly blue eyes. In the picture, Cal gazed intently at his bride, his mouth curling in only the slightest of smiles.

As she set the photo back down a picture of Liam sitting astride a horse caught her eye. Mother of God, he couldn't have been much more than seventeen years old when that photograph was taken. His face was impossibly young and intensely beautiful. He wore a cowboy hat pushed way back on his blond head, and he was laughing. In the background were the gorgeous mountains that surrounded his brother's Montana ranch. Marisala recognized them, even though she'd never been to Montana. Liam had described their beauty to her countless times in both English and Spanish as they lay in the jungle, hiding from the soldiers who were searching for them both.

She opened the top drawer of his dresser, knowing that she shouldn't, but unable to stop herself.

It was filled with a jumble of gleaming white briefs and socks of all colors. She'd found Liam's underwear drawer.

Giggling, Marisala quickly shut it, chastising herself as she turned away. *Make yourself at home* definitely didn't include poking through Liam's underwear drawer.

She moved quickly across the room to turn off the radio. She shouldn't have come in here. Not uninvited. Of course, if she had anything to say about it, it wouldn't be long before she *was* invited in.

As she switched off the music she saw the copy of Salinger's short stories on Liam's bedside table. *Raise High the Roof Beam, Carpenters.* Liam had told her he always went back to his favorite writer, J.D., and that story in particular, whenever he was feeling bad.

Something *was* bothering him. She'd known from the moment she'd seen him at the airport. He was hiding something from her. At first she'd thought that was only the result of time. The years they'd spent apart would naturally put some distance between them.

She picked up the book and there, inside, being used as a bookmark, was an envelope made of a fine off-white linen blend. The same kind of paper her uncle used.

Sure enough, as she turned it over, she saw it was addressed to Liam in Santiago's familiar, spidery handwriting.

Make yourself at home did *not* include reading Liam's mail.

Except the letter *was* from her uncle and probably concerned her. And the temptation to find out exactly what her uncle had said to Liam was too powerful.

Marisala opened the letter and began to read.

THREE

Liam saw her only by chance. Marisala was walking quickly down the street, nearly three blocks away from his condo. Her backpack was over her shoulders, her suitcase in her hand.

What the hell? . . .

He pulled his car in next to a fire hydrant, leaving his flashers on as he ran after her. "Marisala!"

She turned to see him chasing her, then turned away, never even breaking stride.

"Hey," he said, finally catching up to her. "What's the matter? Where are you going?"

She didn't slow down as she glared at him and let loose a volley of Spanish.

His own Spanish had become quite good after two years in San Salustiano, but it had been a long time since he'd used it. He caught the gist of her words, though. Something about sewer rats, horse manure, and him. Something about a letter from Santiago that she'd found and read, something about deceitful, dung-eating former friends . . .

She knew. Somehow, she'd found Santiago's letter, and she *knew*.

Liam swore sharply, running once again to catch up with her. "Marisala, I swear, I was going to tell you—"

She spun to face him then. "Yeah?" she said. "When? When were you going to tell me that Santiago has asked you to teach me how to dress, and how to stand, and how to be quiet when the men are talking? When were you going to mention that he has asked you to teach me how to walk and make small talk and even how I should wear my hair?"

She was furious. She was shaking with indignation, and Liam knew he'd made a mistake. "I'm sorry. I should have told you right away."

"I don't need your help. I don't need a guardian. And I *certainly* don't need your false hospitality."

"Marisala—"

"How could you make such a stupid agreement? How could you even consider doing what Santiago asked?"

"It didn't seem like such a big deal. All you need to do is learn how to come on a little less strong—"

"So I come on too strong?" She all but kicked him in the shins, and Liam knew that she would have liked to. "Thank you so much for informing me of that fact. I had no idea I was so utterly *repugnant*!"

"Marisala, your uncle is from another generation. It would be much easier for you to get along with him if you—"

"If I do *what?* If I sit quietly in the corner and not interrupt when he is speaking, even if I have something important to add? If I wear the dresses and skirts he wants me to wear? Or if I spend the rest of my life with Enrique Morales, a man he paid off to marry me?"

"Paid off? What are you talking a—"

"I was almost married a few years ago."

Liam knew that. He'd been invited to the wedding, but he'd sent his regrets. He'd made up some excuse so he didn't have to go and watch Marisala marry someone else. It hadn't been until Santiago had written to him a few months ago that he'd found out the wedding plans had fallen through.

"A few days before the wedding, I found out Santiago had approached my lover, Enrique. Santiago had offered him a very large sum of money to marry me. I didn't know this when he proposed. I thought—" Marisala raised her shoulders and lifted her chin. "I was foolish, but I found out in time and there was no wedding."

Her lover. Enrique. Liam hated the man, deeply, perversely, not just because he had clearly hurt Marisala, but because he had touched her, loved her. And because she had loved *him* enough to want to marry him.

He forced himself to stop thinking about Enrique Morales, the bastard. He forced himself to banish the pictures that had sprung instantly to mind—pictures of Marisala, dark eyes heavy-lidded with passion, wrapped in another man's arms. . . .

He had to clear his throat before he could speak. "Mara, why don't we go back inside and talk?"

"Because I have absolutely no desire to talk to you, that's why not. Because it's going to get dark soon, and I have to find a place to stay tonight."

Liam felt a flash of frustration that was surely amplified by thoughts of Enrique, thoughts that wouldn't be good and go away. He took a deep breath and worked to keep his voice even. "Okay, I know you're mad. You have a right to be mad. I should have told you. I'm sorry. But just because I made a mistake doesn't mean you're not going to stay with me until we find an—"

She picked up her suitcase and started down the sidewalk. "I have nothing more to say to you. I'm twenty-two years old, I don't need a guardian. I don't need you. 'We' are not going to find *anything* together. Leave me alone."

Liam knew he had to stay calm. Sooner or later Marisala's hot temper would cool, and she would once again see reason. He followed her. "Look, I've got a pizza in the car and I'm parked in front of a hydrant. Let's just—"

"No. It's obvious your loyalties lie with Santiago."

They were creating a scene, right there, as he chased her down the sidewalk. Some of the people passing by were giving them a wide berth, others were lingering, watching their exchange with great interest. Liam blocked Marisala's path, feeling his own temper rising dangerously high despite his best intentions. "Forgive me for wanting to help an old friend."

Lightning blazed from her stormy eyes. "Oh, so what am I? A plate of refried beans? How could you side with him like this?"

He threw up his hands in exasperation. "I was un-aware that a new war had started in San Salustiano with you and Santiago on opposite sides!"

Marisala turned away from him to smile sweetly at a young man walking past them on the sidewalk. "Excuse me. I need a place to stay tonight. I was wondering if you could be so kind as to let me stay with y—"

Liam grabbed her arm and pulled her away from the man. "Marisala! Dammit!"

The man hesitated, glancing warily from Marisala to Liam before walking swiftly on.

"*That's* what you have to learn to stop doing!" His voice was dangerously close to a shout. "That's the kind of behavior that drives Santiago crazy!"

"So *I* have to change," she countered hotly. "But when his behavior drives *me* crazy, that's okay, right? *He* doesn't have to change?"

She sat down suddenly on the front steps of one of the buildings that lined the street. Liam could see the fatigue in her shoulders and back. And he could see that although she tried to hide it, she was more than angry. She was hurt.

"I don't know," she said quietly. "I thought I'd be glad when the war ended. But now that it has, I don't fit in. I want to help make things better in San Salustiano, but I'm not a politician. I wasn't even any good at or-ganizing the students, the way Enrique was."

Enrique again. Liam didn't want to hear that name ever again. Yet at the same time he wanted to know ev-erything about the man.

Marisala shook her head. "And even if I had been

good at politics, there'd be no room for me. A woman running for a position in the government? Yeah, sure. Who'd vote for me? Not even the other women. Most men on the island don't allow their wives to vote."

Liam sat down next to her, his own anger instantly evaporated. He took her hand, linking their fingers together, knowing that the last thing he should do was touch her, but unable to resist.

She glanced over at him, and her eyes were so sad. "I don't fit in," she said again.

"You know, that's what going to college is about," he told her. "Finding out where you fit in, deciding what it is you want to do with your life."

"I already know what I want to do with my life. I want to dress in comfortable clothes and loudly speak my opinion to whomever, *when*ever I want. I want to get Santiago off my back."

"All you need to do to make Santiago happy is learn how to make him see what he wants to see. You need to learn when to keep the conversation only to small talk, when to let other people take the lead, and when to make a point to fix your hair and change into something other than jeans and a T-shirt. You don't have to change. You just have to *seem* to change."

"That's what you do, isn't it? You hide the way you really feel behind your smile." She held tightly to his hand as she looked searchingly into his eyes. "Doesn't it eat you up inside? Doesn't it make you feel like a liar?"

Liam was surprised at her words. A liar? "No," he said. Actually, he'd never thought about it that way before. Hiding the way he really felt . . . "No," he repeated, trying to sound more convincing. "There are times to speak out, and times to . . . just let things go. That's not hiding."

"So that's what you're going to try to teach me, huh?" she asked, looking down at their hands, still clasped together. "How to let things go?"

"The last time we spoke, Santiago told me he's planning to come to Boston in about eight weeks," Liam told her quietly. "If you let me, I can help you learn to show him what he wants to see. I can teach you how to present yourself to him the way he wants to see you. And then you'll have what you want, because he'll get off your back."

"It sounds like surrendering."

"No, it's just winning in a different way."

Marisala sighed. "I don't really have a choice, do I?"

Liam caught her chin with his free hand, forcing her to look into his eyes. "Yes, you do," he said. "With me, you have a choice. Because despite everything you said, we *are* still friends. We'll always be friends. And you know damn well if it ever *did* come to choosing sides between you and Santiago, I'd be the one standing right next to *you*."

Marisala pressed her cheek against the palm of his hand. "I'm sorry I called you a sewer rat who lives in a nest of horse manure."

He pulled his hand away from the silken softness of her face, hiding his sudden rush of emotion and need with a snort of laughter as he stood up. "No, you're not."

But she stood up, too, catching his hand in hers,

bringing it up to the softness of her lips. She kissed his knuckles and the featherlight sensation was totally un-nerving.

But this time he couldn't move away from her. Her lips felt too damn good.

"Yes, I am," she whispered. "I *am* sorry."

When she released his hand, he tried to convince himself that his sudden disappointment was in fact re-lief. But when she stepped even closer and reached up to touch the side of his face, he knew the truth. There was nothing in the world he wanted more than to kiss Marisala.

"We *are* friends," she said again. "When I'm with you, I can say what I want. And you—you can do the same, you know."

"I will," he whispered, and he knew right then that she was right. He *was* a liar. He wanted to kiss her, but he'd never tell her that. He couldn't.

She pulled him close, not for a kiss, but to embrace him in a friendly hug.

He buried his face in the sweet-smelling mass of her beautiful hair. He could feel the softness of her breasts against his chest, feel her fingers lacing through his own hair, feel her thighs pressed against his as she stood on tiptoe.

And he was lost.

He must've lifted her chin, but he didn't remember doing it. He didn't remember leaning closer so that his lips could cover hers, either.

All he knew was that suddenly he was kissing her.

Her lips were so soft, her mouth so deliciously

sweet. All of his longing and need exploded with a savage desperation, and he claimed her mouth, sweeping his tongue past her parted lips, angling his head to kiss her harder, deeper. He wanted to consume her completely, to inhale her, to drink her in.

It was heaven.

His blood surged through his veins as his heart pounded the rhythm of her name and his stomach did crazy, giddy somersaults.

She held him tightly, pressing herself even closer to him as she kissed him just as hungrily, as if she were as starved for his touch as he was for hers.

God help him, he wanted nothing more than to stand there, kissing her, kissing Marisala, lost in her perfect sweetness for the entire rest of his life.

Kissing Marisala . . .

Kissing . . .

Dear God, what was he doing?

Liam took hold of Marisala's narrow shoulders and pushed her to an arm's length. Her eyes were wide and her full lips were swollen from his kisses. She was breathing hard, the white cotton of her shirt moving rapidly up and down with each breath she took.

"That was wrong," he said. He, too, was so out of breath he could barely speak. "That was very wrong. I'm sorry, I shouldn't have—"

"Wrong?" She laughed aloud. "Are you crazy?"

"I'm your guardian, you're my ward. It was *wrong*."

"It was *right*. You're a man, I'm a woman," she countered. "I think you should kiss me again."

"We're friends." Liam's voice sounded desperate to

his own ears, and he tried instead to be rational and calm. "Friends who become lovers don't usually stay friends."

"But—"

He cupped her face with his hands, stopping her words by lightly pressing his thumbs against her lips, afraid he might immediately crumble against any arguments she could make.

"I don't want to use you that way, Mara. You deserve better than me, better than this. You deserve love, *real* love, not this . . . insanity. Please, we have to pretend this didn't happen."

She pulled away from him. "But it *did* happen."

"Please," he said again. "Let's just get into my car and go home and have pizza."

"Pizza."

"Yeah."

"You'd rather have *pizza*."

"Yes," he lied. "Definitely."

She laughed. "Well, then, I guess we'll have pizza. For now."

As he carried her suitcase to his car, as she waited for him to unlock the door, Liam cursed himself for being so damn weak. He'd *kissed* her. He'd sworn it wouldn't happen, yet it had.

And Marisala . . . She was much too quiet.

As Liam put his car into gear and drove home, he had no doubt that she had her own opinions to share on the subject of that kiss. And sooner or later—and probably sooner, knowing Marisala—he was going to hear them.

The phone was ringing as Marisala unlocked the door to Liam's condo and let herself in. "I'll get it," she called, putting the bag of groceries on the long, glass tabletop that held the telephone and setting the puppy on the tile floor.

"Don't—" Liam came thundering down the stairs as she picked up the telephone receiver.

"Hello?" she said. "Bartlett residence."

". . . answer that," he said more quietly, swearing under his breath.

The puppy's enormous feet slipped on the tile, and she skidded, falling onto her fluffy little bottom.

"My God, an actual human voice," said the man on the other end of the line. "Bartlett must not have told you yet not to pick up the phone."

Liam was shaking his head. "I'm not taking calls," he mouthed nearly silently. "I don't want to talk to anyone."

"I'm sorry," Marisala asked into the phone. "Who is this?"

"Buddy Fisher. His agent? Of course, he probably doesn't need an agent anymore, since he seems intent on celebrating the one-year anniversary of his book deadline by *still* not finishing the damned manuscript."

"I'm sorry, Mr. Fisher." Marisala watched as Liam walked in a slow circle around the puppy, who seemed to be thoroughly enjoying her inability to walk without slipping and sliding. "Liam's unavailable."

"Yeah, I *bet* he's unavailable. Listen, honey, tell your

new boyfriend that he's got to deliver the book or cough up the advance money. The publisher's breathing down my neck because Bartlett's stopped answering his phone. Tell him all they want is proof that he's still alive. All they want is his picture on the cover and his promise to make the rounds of the morning talk shows. Tell him I've been talking to a guy named Dave Furth who's willing to ghostwrite the damn thing. Will you please tell him that? I've left Furth's number on Bartlett's machine more than once. If he wants it again, have him call me."

"I'll give him the message."

"Just between you and me, honey, you might want to hang up the phone, give Bartlett the message, and walk out the door. He might be brilliant, handsome as sin, and charismatic as hell, but the man's got some serious problems."

The line was disconnected before Marisala could answer. She hung up the phone. "I think you better start looking for a new agent. When they start telling someone they think is your girlfriend to leave you, you've got to wonder if they're working in your best interest."

"There's a dog in my house."

"He recommended I give you this message and then walk out the door."

"Ah. So he's a *talking* dog."

"The puppy's a she. I'm referring to Buddy Fisher. Your *agent*? Or maybe you don't remember him because you haven't spoken to him in so long."

Liam crouched on the floor. The puppy was looking at him as intently and as skeptically as he was looking at the puppy. "Why is there a dog in my house?"

"Why is your agent calling with the name and phone number of a *ghost*writer?"

Liam held out his finger for the puppy to sniff. "This has got to be the ugliest dog I've ever seen."

Marisala sat down on the floor, and the puppy skittered over toward her, leaping into her lap. "She is *not* ugly. She's gorgeous. Look at those big brown eyes. She's just a little dirty."

"You're right. She's beautiful. I just wanted to get you to stop talking about Fisher. Where'd you find her?"

The puppy's soft baby fur was matted with mud and dirt. She'd clearly been living on the streets, on her own, for some time. "She followed me home from the Star Market."

Liam's eyes narrowed. "You went all the way up to Boylston Street? To the Star Market?"

Marisala narrowed her own eyes back at him. "I didn't realize there's a limit as to how far I can and cannot go while taking an evening walk, Warden Bartlett."

Liam looked away, straightening up. "Sorry."

"Liam, why is your agent trying to hook you up with a ghostwriter? And why would he say all those awful things about you? Are you really almost a year behind with your deadline?"

She could see the muscles working in the side of Liam's jaw. He met her eyes only briefly before he focused all of his attention on the puppy in her lap. "Yes, I am. I'm eleven months, two weeks, and four days behind. And counting. I can tell you the minutes and seconds, too, if you want."

She tried to keep her voice even. "What happened?"

He sat down on the stairs leading up to the bedrooms, rubbing his forehead with one hand. With his face tight and his smile nowhere in sight, he looked tired and haunted and impossibly unhappy.

"I don't know." He closed his eyes, his forehead in the palm of his hand, elbow resting on his knee. "I started writing the damn thing almost four years ago. I wrote about fifteen pages, and then I stopped."

When he opened his eyes, the sudden blueness was almost startling. "I don't want to talk about this, do you mind?" He stood up. "Does the dog have any tags?"

"No." Marisala gently pushed the puppy off her lap and stood up too. "Liam—"

"Don't name her, Mara," he said warningly. "Okay? Don't get too attached. She looks like a purebred cocker spaniel. She's got to belong to somebody, and they're going to want her back. Besides, it's going to be hard enough to find an apartment even if you *don't* have a pet."

He took the bag of groceries off the table and carried it into the kitchen. "Come on," he continued. "She can spend the night in the kitchen. Tomorrow I'll borrow an instant camera. We can take her picture and make flyers to post—let people know you found her."

Marisala picked up the puppy. "The kitchen is going to be so lonely," she said, rubbing her long floppy ears.

"You want to take her upstairs, take her upstairs,"

Liam said, turning back to look at her. "But when she has an accident on the carpet, *you* get to clean it up."

"That's only fair." She followed Liam, wishing he would tell her why he was having such trouble writing his book, wishing he would talk to her, wishing he would kiss her again.

He'd *kissed* her. Mother of God, she still couldn't quite believe that Liam Bartlett had actually *kissed* her.

It had been wildly different from the way she'd imagined their first kiss would be, and she'd imagined it quite frequently since he'd first walked into her uncle's house all those years ago. She'd always thought that he'd gaze into her eyes and slowly move closer, giving her plenty of time to anticipate. She'd pictured him lightly brushing her lips with his, pulling back to look at her again before he gently deepened the kiss.

She'd imagined a sweet, reverent joining of their lips.

Instead he'd possessed her with a fierceness that had melted her bones and infused her with a raging fire. She'd exploded, responding with years of pent-up longing. Saints help her, she'd damn near wrapped her leg around him in an attempt to pull him even closer.

He wanted her. She knew now that it was true. The unmistakable and impossibly quick response of his body as he pressed against her proved that without a doubt, didn't it?

His blood burned for her, making him hot and hard as stone. No one—*no* one—could resist a passion that strong.

Not even Liam Bartlett, Patron Saint of San Salustiano.

"Is the dog hungry?" Liam asked as she set the
puppy down on the kitchen floor.

"No," Marisala told him. "I gave her some of the
cold cuts I bought at the market."

Liam laughed. "No wonder she followed you."

"She followed me before that."

"But no doubt the cold cuts cemented the deal. God,
you are such a pushover when it comes to strays." The
newspaper was out and open to the apartment listings
on the kitchen table. Liam took several of the pages
from another section and handed them to Marisala.
"You might try spreading this out on the floor of the
bathroom that's attached to your room. Here's hoping
she's at least a little trained."

Marisala leaned over the table, looking closely at the
newspaper. "You've circled some of these listings."

"There's not a lot that were suitable. I marked only
a few."

"Here's one that you didn't mark that looks good.
It's in the price range we were talking about, and it says
'near university.' "

"Where?" Liam leaned over Marisala's shoulder.

"Here." She pointed to the listing, reading aloud.
" 'Near university. Studio with separate kitchen, utilities
included. B-S-M-T of house.' What's B-S-M-T?"

She turned to look at him and their faces were suddenly only inches apart.

Liam quickly straightened up. "Basement," he told

her. "Believe me, you don't want to live in a basement apartment."

Marisala shrugged. "I've lived in far worse." She turned again to face him and he jumped back, away from her, over to the other side of the kitchen. The puppy jumped too, startled.

"Is there a problem with the way I smell?" she asked, lifting one eyebrow. "Should I take a shower?"

Liam shot an exasperated glance at her. "I'm just . . ." He took a deep breath and started over as he began putting away the groceries she'd bought. "I just think it would be smarter if we kept our distance. From each other. You know."

Marisala nodded. At least he was being honest. At least he wasn't trying to pretend that they both didn't know he was jumpy as hell because she was around. Because of that kiss. "Maybe we should talk about what happened today."

"There's nothing to say." Liam folded the paper bag and slid it between the refrigerator and the wall. That done, he started to pace. Marisala was beginning to wonder if he ever stood still.

"I disagree."

He pressed the bridge of his nose with his fingers as if he had a headache. "It's late. Maybe we should just go to bed."

"Well, that's an interesting solution. Your room or mine?"

Liam spun to face her. "Mara!"

"I was making a joke. You've got to . . . what's that expression you always used to use on me? *Lighten up.*"

He sat down at the table, but even then he didn't stop moving. He touched the pepper mill and salt-shaker. He rearranged the napkins in the napkin holder. "Maybe we *should* talk."

"Okay." She sat down across from him and folded her hands demurely in front of her. "I'll go first. I liked the way you kissed me."

He closed his eyes. "God, how did I know you weren't going to make this easy for me?"

"There's nothing easy or hard about this," she countered. "You kissed me. I kissed you. Either you liked it or you didn't."

"Yeah, well, I didn't."

At first his words stung, but then she realized she could still see the fiery remnants of that same burning passion in his eyes.

So she lifted her chin and laughed. "You are *such* a liar. You liked it as much as I did. Maybe even more."

Liam ran his hands down his face. "Okay, yeah. You're right. I liked it, but I *didn't* like it. As much as it made me feel good, it made me feel bad too." He sighed noisily, briefly closing his eyes. When he opened them again, he stared down at the kitchen floor. "I don't think of you as a woman, Mara. To me, you'll always be a child. A little girl. A sister. Someone to protect, not take advantage of. Not someone to kiss." He gazed across the table then, looking her squarely in the eye. "I love you dearly, kid, but not *that* way."

He didn't think of her as a woman. Marisala had been prepared to argue with Liam all night if necessary, but she couldn't think of a single thing to say to counter *that*.

"And I'm sorry if I led you to believe—"

She interrupted him, suddenly wanting nothing more than to have this conversation over with. "No. You didn't. I mean, I didn't. Believe *any*thing, really, I mean . . ." She took a deep breath and even managed to smile. "I guess I just thought it would be really special. You know, you and me."

The look in his eyes was unreadable as he nodded. "We've already got something really special."

Marisala nodded, pushing her chair out from the table. The puppy looked up at her expectantly, and she bent to scoop her up. "I'll see you in the morning." She tucked the extra sheets of newspaper under her arm.

"Oh, yeah, that reminds me." He stood up too. "I've got some things to take care of downtown in the morning. Why don't you sleep in, and we can check out some of these apartments after lunch?"

It was amazing. He was acting so casual and friendly, as if he hadn't just smashed all of her blazing hopes into tiny, unrecognizable pieces. Marisala felt sick to her stomach, and *he* was making plans for tomorrow.

"That's fine," she murmured. "I'll see you then."

She went up the stairs and down the hall to her bedroom, wondering at this odd queasiness that made her chest ache. If she didn't know better, if she weren't so sure that her feelings for Liam were based only on years of friendship and sheer physical attraction, she might've thought that once again he'd managed to break her heart.

FOUR

"This isn't the best neighborhood in the city."

Marisala looked at Liam over the top of his car. "That's what you said about the *last* apartment we looked at."

"Yeah, that was a real dump too."

"It wasn't that bad."

"The living-room window had a view of a brick wall. Three feet away, there *was* a brick wall. And the entry-way door didn't lock. Anyone could get in."

"I lived in the jungle for nearly four years," she reminded him. "Compared to some of the places I spent the night, that apartment was not bad."

"I'd never sleep," he told her as they walked toward the next address on her list. "I would be up until dawn, worrying about you. What's the street number of this next place?"

"Five thirty-two. The landlord's in Apartment Two." Marisala glanced at the lines of fatigue on Liam's face. As it was, he hadn't slept much last night. She'd heard him moving around quite late and had gotten up to see the lights blazing throughout the rest of the condo.

She wondered if he had nightmares. *She* still did. She couldn't imagine anyone living through what they had and *not* being haunted by it for the rest of their lives. But Liam had also survived all those months in prison, suffering God only knew what kind of mistreatment and abuse. She'd seen the scars on his back from the countless beatings. She could only guess what other scars he bore as well—both inside and out.

God knows she had her own scars.

Marisala caught sight of the crescent-shaped mark on her left cheekbone in the glimmering reflection from a newly washed car window. She'd always considered that scar a badge of her tremendous good luck. She had been struck by flying shrapnel. Had it hit her a few centimeters higher, she would have lost her eye. And if her head had been slightly turned, it could well have hit her in the temple, where even a glancing blow might have killed her.

But now, as she saw herself reflected in the car window, she saw the way the scar interrupted the smooth lines of her face. And while she had always scoffed at her uncle's suggestion that a plastic surgeon might be able to make the scar smaller and less noticeable, Liam hadn't seemed to think the idea was so farfetched.

Maybe such a large scar on her face made Liam find her unattractive. Less womanly.

Marisala glanced at him as they climbed the stairs to

the porch of a three-family house and rang the land-lord's bell. He was wearing a funky pair of mirrored sunglasses that hid his eyes and made his face unread-able.

"After this, I'm taking you to a realtor," Liam told her. "They'll find you a *real* apartment."

"But I'll have to pay a fee of a half month's rent."

"I'll pay it," he said shortly. "I'll pay for the whole damn thing if I have to."

Mother of God, he was eager to be rid of her. Marisala kept her face carefully expressionless, trying to conceal the anger and frustration that boiled inside of her. What had happened to their easygoing friendship? What had become of the man who had once trusted her enough to put his life in her hands? Who was this stiff stranger who stood in front of her now? "Well, it will be good to be settled. Classes start on Monday." Her voice shook slightly, giving her away. He glanced at her, and she knew he could tell how badly his words hurt her.

Liam rang the bell again, and when he spoke, his voice was softer, as if he were trying to make up for sounding so hard. "Tonight we can look at your sched-ule, and I'll take you around and show you where your classes are."

"You don't—"

"—have to do that, I know." Liam managed a small, slightly crooked smile. "I got your refrain down cold, babe. But you should know mine by heart now as well."

"You don't have to do it, but you *want* to," Marisala recited. She paused. "You don't *look* like you want to do much besides go home and crawl into bed."

"I had a rough night."

Marisala's frustration and anger eased with her empathy toward those flatly spoken words. She knew what it was to have a rough night. It was funny, some nights she could sleep like a baby. But others, the nightmares hovered on the fringes of her consciousness and she didn't dare close her eyes until she was so exhausted she knew a dreamless sleep would come.

"Do you want to talk about it?" she asked softly.

He didn't look at her, didn't even hesitate. "No."

The word came out flatly, almost rudely, but Marisala only felt more compassion. It was her experience that sometimes men had it worse. Some men found it terribly difficult to handle the fear and panic that the nightmares would bring. "I'm here if you ever change your mind."

He didn't get a chance to answer as the door opened and the landlord stepped onto the porch. "You're here to see the apartment? The entrance is around this way."

The unkempt-looking man led the way around to the side of the house. Marisala let Liam follow first as the man rattled off a list of rules about rent, utilities, parking unavailability, pets, and noise.

No pets. Of course, Liam was probably right about the puppy. She *had* to belong to someone. They'd stopped at the copy shop and posted some flyers in the local stores before embarking on today's great apartment hunt. There was probably a message from the puppy's owner on Liam's answering machine right now.

The landlord stopped at a door in the side of the building and searched for the key. Unlocking the door, he opened it, gesturing for Liam to go in first. "There's a light switch at the bottom of the stairs."

But Liam stopped short, and Marisala nearly smashed her nose against his wide and very solid back.

"It's a *basement* apartment," he said.

"That's what makes it affordable." Marisala moved past him, going down into the darkness. The landlord had told her over the phone this morning that even though not much light came in through the narrow ceiling-high windows, the rooms were dry. They were cool in the summer and warm in the winter.

She found the light and switched it on.

It certainly was gloomy, a fact that could be helped by painting over the drab and dingy yellowish-beige walls with bright whites and festive colors. The floor was covered with impossibly ugly beige vinyl tiles and the ceilings were low. Liam would have to duck to keep from bumping his head when he came into the room.

"Marisala." Liam was still standing outside the door. "You can't live in a basement apartment."

The place was small, but certainly in much better shape than the last few apartments they'd looked at. She could definitely live here, basement or not.

"It's not bad," she called up to him.

"Mara . . ."

"Kitchen's in the back, bathroom's off that." The landlord pushed past Liam to come down the stairs. He opened a door. "Here's your closet. The other door provides access to the oil burner. If there's ever a problem, repairmen would need to get in there, so I'd have to ask you not to put any furniture in front of that doorway."

Furniture. God, she was going to have to get furniture—at least a bed, and a table to use for studying and eating her meals.

Marisala wandered back into the kitchen.

"Mara," Liam's voice called after her. "Dammit!"

There was a window in the kitchen, too, but again, little light came through the glass. She looked at it closely, wondering if a good washing might help.

The landlord came in behind her and switched on the overhead light. Liam was right behind him. "Mara, let's go. There's no way you can live here. It's too . . . small."

It *was* small. The kitchen could barely hold the three of them.

"Hey, look. It's got a microwave." Marisala turned toward the landlord. "Does this come with the place?"

"Yeah, see, there's no regular oven."

"How does it work?"

"Just make sure the door's latched, turn the dial to the time, and press start."

Marisala pressed start, and the appliance hummed.

"Mara." There was something, an added intensity or urgency in Liam's voice that made her look over her shoulder as she went into the tiny bathroom and turned on the light. "It's too *small*. Let's *go*."

The muscles were working in Liam's jaw as he clenched his teeth. He was stony-faced and unsmiling, his cheekbones standing out in sharp relief. There were actually beads of sweat above his upper lip. That was odd. It wasn't all that hot in here.

"Liam, are you all—"

The lights went out. With the sudden pop of a blown fuse, they were plunged into gloomy darkness.

The landlord cursed. "The microwave's on the same current as the bathroom fan and the load's too much for it. I've got to get that fixed. The box is up in my apartment. I'll be right back."

"Mara, I can't stand it. We have to get out of here," Liam said hoarsely. He was little more than a shadowy shape in the gloom. *"Right now."*

She understood then. In a flash, it was absolutely clear. He'd spent close to eighteen months of his life in a cell, certainly underground, and probably in the dark. "Go," she said. "Quickly."

His voice was tight. "I can't leave you here."

"I'm right behind you," she said, moving toward him.

She heard him bolt for the door, heard him stumble as he went up the stairs, heard the door slam open as he pushed his way outside.

Marisala followed as quickly as she could and found him leaning against his car, both hands braced on the hood, head down. "Are you okay?"

"Yeah." His eyes were closed and he was still breathing hard. He was shaking, but when she reached for him, he pulled away. "Don't. Just give me a minute, will you?"

He was ashamed. She saw the tinge of pink across his cheeks. She could almost feel his mortification.

He sat down, right there on the curb, trying hard to slow his breathing.

Marisala sat down next to him, careful not to touch him. "Why didn't you just wait outside?"

He turned to look at her then, anger and shame still glistening in his eyes. "Because I didn't want you alone in there with that guy. He gave me the creeps."

He'd gone in there for her. He'd known what going down those stairs would do to him, and yet he'd done it anyway. For her. He'd done it because she was too stupid to figure out why exactly he was so adamant that she not rent a basement apartment.

How could she have been so insensitive? It didn't take much to realize he'd spent nearly a year and a half underground. "I'm so sorry. I wasn't thinking."

Liam shook his head. "It's no big deal. So I can't handle basements. So what?"

They sat for a moment in silence.

"You never told me," Marisala said finally, "about all those months you spent in the prison. You told your brother about it, didn't you?"

"No."

"You *did* talk to *some*one? . . . "

Liam shook his head. "I didn't want to talk about it. I still don't. I don't want to *think* about it."

"Mother of God, Liam, you just can't pretend it didn't happen."

"You wanna bet?"

"No," she said, purposely taking him literally. "I don't want to bet. I want you to find someone to talk to about this. If it's still affecting you this way after all these years—"

He pushed himself to his feet. "Look, all I have to do is stay out of basements."

"And elevators?" she guessed.

He shrugged, but the movement served only to emphasize the tension in his shoulders. "It's no big deal."

"And how about the nightmares?" she asked quietly. She knew from the look on his face that she'd guessed correctly. He slept badly—when he slept at all. "Or maybe you just figure it's natural to sleep only two or three out of every seven nights."

He turned away from her. "It's not that bad. I sleep. Some of the time."

Marisala stood up too. "What if it does get that bad? What then? Will you try to ignore that too?"

He dragged his hand through his hair. "Look, why don't you wait until *after* you take freshman psychology before you start playing shrink?"

Her temper flared. "I was there in San Salustiano too," she told him tightly. "Remember? I may not have been in the prison, but I know what it's like to be afraid of it. I spent years wondering what would happen if I were taken prisoner—whether I'd be strong enough to survive."

He backed down instantly. "I know. I'm sorry."

"Yeah, you should be. I'm only trying to be your friend. And I'm going to *keep* trying. Unless you've decided that you don't want to be friends with a *child* anymore."

He looked at her then and smiled, but she knew it

was just part of his disguise. Inside, he was not smiling. It was possible that he hadn't really smiled in years. "Don't get cute."

"That's my problem, remember? I don't know how to be cute. That's one of the things you're going to have to teach me."

Liam laughed, and for one heart-stopping moment, Marisala was certain he was going to pull her into his arms. But instead, he turned away. "Let's go try to find you a *real* apartment."

Liam woke up to the jarringly festive sound of salsa music.

He sat straight up, eyes instantly open but brain still befuddled. Where the hell was he? And what the hell was that music?

It didn't take more than a few bleary blinks of his eyes for him to recognize his bedroom. And as for the music . . .

Marisala must've been in his room. She must've come in and changed the station on his clock radio and . . .

There was a long, dark strand of hair on one of his pillows. Liam had a sudden flash of memory of Marisala in his bed, minus her clothing, her lithe body smooth as silk beneath his eager fingers, her body arching upward as his mouth claimed one perfect, pebbled nipple.

Holy God, had she come into his room last night and climbed into his bed and? . . .

No. No, it had only been in his dreams that he and Marisala had made incredible, decadently erotic love.

He sank back against his pillows, closing his eyes, willing away the images that had made him instantly aroused. He didn't know which was worse, dreaming about the prison, or dreaming about Marisala. Either way, he was destined to wake up gasping for air.

On the radio, the deejay announced that it was going to be another hot one.

The man was speaking Spanish, and Liam understood nearly every word. It was funny how quickly it came back to him. Not that he wanted it to. He'd just as soon forget it all. The war, San Salustiano, his Spanish, *everything*.

Even Marisala. Maybe *especially* Marisala.

Liam reached for the clock radio and shut it off as he rolled out of bed. He showered quickly and pulled on a clean pair of shorts and a polo shirt. Today they were destined to find Marisala an apartment. They *had* to. Classes started in a matter of days.

And it was only a matter of time before she realized that crap he'd told her about thinking of her as a child was just that—crap. Then she *would* come sneaking into his room at night, and he wouldn't be able to resist her, and their entire friendship—as well as his friendship with her uncle—would be in jeopardy.

The smell of fresh coffee brewing wafted through the air as he started down the stairs.

Liam braced himself as he headed toward the kitchen. It was still early—he wouldn't put it past Marisala to have come down to grab a quick cup of coffee while still in her nightclothes. She probably slept in an oversized T-shirt, her long, tanned legs bare, God help him.

But as he went into the kitchen he saw that Marisala was dressed. She wore baggy knee-length, cutoff shorts slung low on her waist and a midriff-baring tank top that revealed a small tattoo high up on her left arm. It was a single flame—the symbol of the San Salustiano Freedom Fighters. He remembered the first time he'd seen it—after she'd broken him out of the government prison. With the tattoo and the fresh, jagged scar on her beautiful face, and the way she held an AK-47 as if it were an extension of her body, he'd wept for the loss of her youth and innocence.

She was talking as he came in, leaning against the kitchen counter with a mug in one hand, part of the Sunday paper in her other, speaking in her native Spanish.

It took him a moment to realize that she wasn't talking to him, or even to the puppy, who was happily tearing at a clean rag with her sharp little teeth.

Marisala was talking to the man and woman who were sitting at his kitchen table. They were both ragged and dirty, and the woman was heavily pregnant.

Liam did a double take. Where the hell had *they* come from? But he knew the answer before Marisala even turned to greet him. She had gone out for another walk this morning and come home with two more strays.

"*Buenos dias*," Marisala said cheerfully. "You actually slept last night."

He had. He'd fallen asleep some time after two A.M., and he'd stayed asleep, dreaming those intensely erotic dreams about Marisala.

Her hair was loose in a wild cloud of curls around her head, just the way she'd worn it in his dreams. He went toward the cabinet to get himself a mug, unable to meet her gaze for fear she'd be able to read his mind.

"It looks like you've been busy," he said levelly.

"Your column in the paper," she accused him, "it's something you wrote months ago."

"Yeah." He couldn't even glance at her. "I didn't have the time to write something new this week."

"*Por favor, Señor Bartlett.*" The extremely pregnant woman pushed back her chair and hauled herself clumsily to her feet. "Sit. Please. You will allow me to get your coffee and breakfast, no?"

"No," Liam said firmly. "Thank you. You look like you need to sit down more than I do."

"But—" The young woman looked from Liam to Marisala in alarm.

Liam poured himself a cup of coffee as Marisala spoke to the couple in a low voice. He turned to face her. "So. I see you've hired me a cook." It was all he could do not to laugh. Trust Marisala to find two needy, desperate people living on the street and offer them not only food and shelter, but a way for them to keep their pride.

On closer examination, he saw that the man and the woman were both impossibly young. The man was in his early twenties at the most and the girl hardly more than a baby herself.

"Liam, I'd like you to meet Inez and Hector Perez. They came from Puerto Rico, via New York. They are here in Boston looking to get away from . . . certain family troubles."

Liam glanced at Inez's tautly rounded belly. Family troubles indeed.

"And yes, you're right. I told them you might be interested in hiring them. Inez tells me she's quite a good cook," Marisala continued.

Hector was gazing grimly down at the table, embarrassment tingeing his aristocratic cheekbones. Liam could relate. It was never easy to take charity. God knows he'd taken more than his share down in San Salustiano.

"How about you, Mr. Perez," he asked the young man directly. "What's your trade?"

"I am a landscaper."

Liam nodded. A landscaper. If Marisala had her way, he was about to become, no doubt, the very first in his condo association to have his own personal landscaper—without owning even a single handful of dirt to landscape.

"When's the baby due?"

Marisala spoke up. "They're not exactly sure. I'd guess it's a matter of only a week or two."

Liam took a sip of his coffee, nodding again.

She was watching him, a small smile playing about the corners of her mouth. She knew damn well that he wasn't going to toss these people back onto the street a week or two before their baby was due to be born. "I thought . . . well, you have so many extra empty rooms here. . . ."

He gazed back at her over the top of his coffee mug. "And you've already shown the Perezes to theirs, I assume?"

She laughed. But she had. He could see it in her eyes. "You're right. I did. So, can they stay? Or are you going to make me beg?"

Last night in his dreams he'd made her beg. Liam held her gaze much longer than he should have, giving himself a few short seconds to lose himself in the midnight swirl of her eyes. "No," he said quietly. "I won't make you beg." He sat down at the table, across from Hector. "Mr. Perez, I'm afraid I don't need a landscaper at this moment, but I *do* need a cook's assistant. It seems *my* cook is going to have a baby within the next few weeks, and I'd like her to stay off her feet. So, tell me honestly, how's *your* cooking?"

FIVE

"You don't have to come with me," Marisala said.

Liam snorted. "Are you kidding? If I let you go by yourself, God only knows how many more people you'll bring with you when you come home."

"Very funny."

"I'm not kidding," he said, but he was smiling.

Marisala tried to keep her heart from flipping. Tried and failed. Liam Bartlett's smile had always made her heart do somersaults.

If she hadn't known about his writing troubles, about his problems sleeping, and about his near-crippling claustrophobia, she never would have guessed he was dealing with such pressure.

He looked incredible.

He was wearing shorts and an expensive-looking muted pink polo shirt. His legs were tan and strong, and covered with crisp, gleaming blond hair. The scar he had near his left knee was noticeable, but well faded. It could well have been the result of a sports injury or a car accident—not the handiwork of an M60 submachine gun. With his tousled golden hair and the sunglasses he'd already put on, he looked utterly American—well rested, well fed, wealthy, and carefree.

She alone knew of the deep scars that surely still marked his broad, muscular back, souvenirs of the beatings he'd endured at the hands of officials in San Salustiano's so-called democratic government.

As they reached the bottom of the stairs Liam held the door open for her. He was wearing a hint of a familiar tangy cologne. He smelled clean and deliciously fresh.

In turn, Marisala held open the door that led to the sidewalk. It was humid and still outside, the heat from the hazy sun reflecting and magnified by the city streets. "I meant to tell you—a call came in for you while you were in the shower. Your machine picked up, and I couldn't help but overhear. It was a woman. Someone named Lauren?"

She tried to sound casual. Nonchalant. And certainly not as if she were digging for information.

"Hi, Lee," the woman had said as she'd left her message in a breathless, husky, much-too-sexy voice. "It's me, Lauren. We need to talk. Call me at home tonight. Or better yet, stop by my place at around nine? See you then."

"Thanks," Liam said, telling Marisala nothing.

Marisala had to know. "Is she your girlfriend?"

Liam glanced at her, his eyes hidden behind his dark glasses. "She's a friend," he said. "A lady friend."

"Are you sleeping with her?"

"There," he said, stopping her right in the middle of the sidewalk. "You've just given me a perfect example of going too far. That was a question *not* to ask. Whether or not Lauren Stuart and I have a sexual relationship is none of your business."

Lauren Stuart. Liam's "lady friend's" full name was Lauren Stuart. She sounded like a real New England WASP, tall and blonde and elegant—everything Marisala was not. Marisala couldn't squelch her jealousy. "Your life's not my business? Forgive me, I thought we were friends."

"We *are* friends. But even with friends, you have to learn not to blurt out any old question that pops into your mind."

"That wasn't 'any old question.' It was a specific question for which I wanted to know the answer. I wouldn't have asked you something so personal if I hadn't spent more weeks than *you* can remember changing your bedpan, amigo."

"I'm not so sure of that."

"Believe me, it *was* weeks."

"I'm not talking about the bedpans, I'm talking about you saying whatever you want, *when*ever you want. *That's* what you need to work on, and I want you to start by practicing with me."

"But in the jungle—"

"Our friendship is different here than it was in the jungle. Back then, Mara, we shared everything, even after I stopped needing bedpan service. Clothes, blankets—the food we ate." He looked at her over the tops of his sunglasses and tried to get her to smile. "Sometimes we shared the food we ate long after we ate it. Remember Rafe's famous beans? Living in such close quarters, we shared more than we should have."

They *had* shared just about everything—except for what she truly wanted. They hadn't shared their need for physical comfort, for physical love. As they'd spent night after night in that tiny shelter, Marisala had ached for him to kiss and touch her. She had longed for him to temporarily transport her away from the death and destruction they lived with, day in and day out.

But he never had.

It was true, she had been only seventeen and still inexperienced when Liam had left the island. She hadn't known what love could be between a man and a woman. If she had, she would have convinced him—somehow—to share such a miracle with her.

"Is she beautiful, this Lauren? May I ask that?"

"Yes, and yes. She's a very beautiful woman."

Woman. Lauren was a woman, while Marisala was not—at least not in Liam's eyes. He still thought of her as a child.

And it was only a matter of time before she woke up in the night to hear the soft sounds of female laughter as Liam brought this beautiful Lauren Stuart up to his room. It was only a matter of time before Marisala came face-to-face with Liam's lover over the breakfast table.

She glanced at her watch. If they didn't hurry, they were going to be late for her appointment. And suddenly her search for an apartment of her own seemed imperative—moving out of Liam's condo was of the utmost urgency.

"I'm sorry," Liam said to the goatee-wearing young man who'd shown them into an extremely cluttered living room. Dan. He'd introduced himself as Dan. "I think maybe I've misunderstood. You're *not* moving out of this place?"

"He's renting out only *one* of the rooms," Marisala explained. "See, this house has four bedrooms—"

"Five," Dan interjected.

"And one of them is empty. For only two hundred and fifty dollars a month, I could become a housemate. I'd have to share the kitchen and living areas, but—"

"Hey, we're friendly." Dan smiled at Marisala. His teeth were straight and white. "No one bites—at least not too hard. Come on, you want to see the room?"

"Are you a student, Dan?" Liam followed them. He hated this. Marisala moving into a house with strange people—one of them being this man—was a bad idea.

"I'm in law school. Northeastern." Dan answered him politely, but then turned back to Marisala as he led the way up a flight of stairs. "I hope you like the room. You're exactly what we've been looking for. You'll have to meet the others, but I think they'll fall in love with you right away too. I can't believe you're actually from San Salustiano. That was some intense stuff that was going on there a few years back. That's Ed's room. He's in law school with me." Dan pointed to the open doorways of the rooms they passed. "And this one's Bill and

Jodie's. Bill plays bass in a rock band, and Jodie's a potter. Deede's in here. She teaches over at the League School. This is my room, and this one would be yours."

Dan pushed open the last door at the end of the hallway with a flourish.

Marisala's "room" was right next to Dan's. Now, wasn't *that* damned convenient?

"I remember you said on the phone you're a freshman over at the university," Dan continued as he followed Marisala into the empty little room. "This place is just a short ride from the campus."

It was tiny. There wasn't enough room for Liam to go in, too, so he stood in the doorway, looking in, feeling his frustration mounting.

"I'd have to get a bed," Marisala mused. "But not a big one—it wouldn't fit."

She moved toward the window at the end of the room.

Backlit the way she was, with the light coming in through the window, she looked unearthly and angelic. Her dark hair took on gleaming overtones and her face looked so sweet, Liam's chest ached.

He hated the way Dan was looking at her with barely hidden, very male appreciation in his eyes. It wasn't disrespectful, though. On the contrary, Dan seemed very nice. But Liam knew from the look on the man's face that Dan wouldn't be satisfied with having Marisala as only a housemate.

Not that he blamed Dan. There was no doubt about it, Marisala *was* extraordinarily beautiful. And nice. And funny and smart and kind and . . .

And her lips were so soft and her mouth was so kissable, it took all that Liam had to keep himself from dragging her into his arms and kissing her again. He wanted to kiss her until she melted against him and gazed up at him with eyes heavy-lidded with heat and desire—until Dan got the hint and never, *ever* looked at her so hungrily again.

Dan was talking. Apparently the man never shut up. He was going on and on about weekend parties and going out to see Bill or whoever's band play and playing basketball on Tuesday nights over at the roommate named Deede's school gym.

Marisala was listening, nodding, smiling up into Dan's hazel eyes, and something inside of Liam snapped. "This isn't going to work." His voice came out sounding much sharper and rougher than he'd intended.

Both Marisala and Dan turned to look at him in surprise, almost as if they'd forgotten he was standing there.

"Mara, we better go. I'm sorry, Dan. We've wasted your time."

Dan looked from Marisala to Liam and back again. "But—"

"Santiago would never let you live here." Liam knew the moment it was out of his mouth that it was absolutely *the* most wrong thing in the world to say.

Marisala's chin came up and her eyes sparked, and she turned to face Dan. "I'm interested. Tell me, what's the next step?"

"If you're free, you could come back tonight and

meet everyone. In fact, you're welcome to come for dinner—"

Liam stepped forward. "Sorry, Marisala's busy tonight." That was also the wrong thing to say, but once he'd started, he couldn't seem to stop.

Dan lifted an eyebrow. "I think I asked Marisala—not you," he said coolly, straightening to his full height as he gazed at Liam.

There was real strength in the young man's unswerving gaze. He may not have been as tall as Liam. He may not have been as solidly built. But he wasn't about to let anyone push him—or Marisala—around. That much was clear from the set of his shoulders.

In any other situation, Liam would have liked Dan. They probably would have been friends. But right now all he wanted to do was to slam his fist into the younger man's face. Thankfully, he was able to resist that urge, but he was unable to stop himself from taking a threatening step forward. "I answered for her," he told Dan tightly. "As her guardian, I'm telling her right now that this is not the right apartment."

Dan didn't back down. In fact, he stepped forward, too, moving slightly as if his intention was to protect Marisala from Liam. "I don't know where *you're* from, pal, but this is America. And Marisala looks old enough to me to make her own decisions."

Seeing this kid act as if *Liam* were the one Marisala needed protection from was outrageous. And when Dan met Marisala's eyes and smiled reassuringly, Liam laughed out loud.

"Keep your pants zipped, Dan. She hasn't moved in yet."

Marisala's mouth dropped open. She couldn't believe what she had just heard Liam say. Despite the smile on his face, his eyes were steely cold and he was staring at Dan as if he wanted to break him in half.

What was wrong with him? She'd never seen him like this before. If she didn't know better, she would think that he was jealous.

Jealous?

Mother of God, he *was* jealous. Liam was actually *jealous*.

The confusion that hit her was so overwhelming, she couldn't do more than allow herself to be dragged along when Liam took her hand and none too gently pulled her with him out of the room.

If he was *jealous*, that meant . . .

"Marisala, I don't know who this guy is, but you don't have to put up with this." Dan was following them, concern in his pretty green eyes. "If you need some kind of help—"

"I have to apologize for Liam," Marisala called back to Dan as Liam all but threw her over his shoulder and carried her out the front door. "He's been taking this guardian thing much too seriously. He thinks just because my uncle asked him for a favor, he's got to—"

The screen door slammed behind them as Liam pulled her by the wrist across the porch and down the steps to the sidewalk and his car.

". . . he's got to pretend that this fire we feel every

time he touches me doesn't exist," Marisala finished in a much softer voice.

He tried to drop her hand, but this time she was the one who wouldn't let go. He closed his eyes. "Marisala, don't."

He wouldn't look at her and she knew with a flash of triumph that he couldn't. If he did, she'd see all of the desire and longing he was trying so hard to hide.

"You're jealous," she said, still unable fully to believe it herself. "You're jealous of Dan."

"No," Liam said, but he didn't sound very convinced as he finally pulled free from her grasp.

Up at the house, Dan had come out onto the porch. He lit a cigarette and pretended he was out there to smoke, but it was obvious he was there to watch them.

Liam unlocked the passenger door of his car and opened it wide. "Just get in."

"You don't want me to live there because you think Dan wants to be my lover."

He glanced up at the house, up at Dan, and the muscles in the side of his jaw jumped. "I *know* that's what he wants."

"I think you're wrong. I think you're projecting what *you* want onto him."

He closed his eyes as if doing so would keep him from understanding her words. "What I *want* is for you to get into the car."

"Would it really be that terrible?" She brought his hand to her lips then pressed the softness of his palm against her cheek. "You know, you and me?"

He stood very, very still.

"We used to be honest with each other," she whispered. "Why should we lie about this?"

Liam turned toward her then, and for the first time since she saw him at the airport, he let her truly look into his eyes. "I don't know what the truth is anymore. Everything's so complicated."

"It doesn't have to be."

"I can't change the way I feel. And the thought of acting upon this . . . attraction"—he had trouble getting the word out—"feels really wrong to me."

"Maybe it would simplify things."

He pulled away from her, exhaling loudly. It was almost a laugh. "I doubt that."

From the porch, Dan called, "Marisala, is everything all right?"

"She's fine," Liam called back. "Everything's fine."

Everything was *not* fine. How could he say that?

Liam turned to her, all of the fire and pain in his eyes once again carefully concealed. "Please. Just get in the car."

She did, setting her bag on the floor beneath her legs and fastening the seat belt.

This was what Liam was supposed to teach her. This was what Santiago wanted her to learn to do. He wanted her to learn to smile and say that everything was fine, even when it wasn't. *Especially* when it wasn't.

Liam got in beside her and started the engine with a roar.

He was so wrong. If they became lovers, if he came to her room tonight, the entire world and all of its problems would disappear. There would be only Liam and only Marisala, together in the simplicity of their shared pleasure and passion.

She glanced at him as he drove. His jaw was tight, his mouth a thin line. He kept his eyes firmly on the road, as if he were afraid to meet her gaze.

And he *was* afraid, she realized. He was terrified of the palpable attraction that flared to life between them whenever their eyes met, whenever they were even in the same room.

And she knew with absolute certainty that it was only a matter of time before she broke through his defenses—particularly since they were sharing his condo.

Even though just that morning Marisala had longed to find her own apartment, she now wished fervently for the opposite. With any luck, she'd never find a place good enough or clean enough or safe enough to satisfy Liam.

"Hey, check it out." Liam hit the brakes and pulled sharply to the side of the road.

Out in front of one of the triple-decker houses that lined the side street a man was making adjustments to a sign that was standing in the tiny yard. In large red letters, it read, APARTMENT FOR RENT.

Liam lowered Marisala's window with the push of one button and leaned across her to call to the man. "Excuse me! Are you putting that up or taking it down?"

"Up," the man said, his gaze flicking over Liam's expensive car. "You looking? I could show you the place right now if you want."

"It's not a basement apartment, is it?" Marisala asked hopefully.

"Nope. Second floor. One bedroom. Nice and bright."

"Excellent." Liam pulled up the parking brake. "Is this luck, or is this luck?" he asked Marisala as he put the window back up and shut off the engine.

Unfortunately, it no longer was the kind of luck she was hoping for. She climbed out of Liam's car, knowing with a sense of ironic resignation that this apartment was going to be absolutely perfect.

It was.

It was clean, it was bright, it was well kept, and it was within her price range. There were no bugs, no holes in the wall, no leaky sinks or blocked plumbing.

It was, however, currently occupied.

Liam pulled her aside in the kitchen. "I think you should tell this guy yes right now. If you wait, even a few hours, this apartment'll be gone."

"When do you need to move in?" the landlord called from the living room. "The current tenants told me they'd stay until October fifteenth if I couldn't find a new tenant by then. I know they'd probably be willing to move out a few weeks earlier if you needed to get in here. They're definitely going to be here until the end of September, but you could probably move in on October first if that's convenient."

October first was an entire month away. Marisala felt a surge of hope. Maybe . . .

Liam was shaking his head as he went into the living room. "We really need something immediately, but . . ." He looked around, then glanced back at Marisala. "What do you think? Could you stand to wait until October first?"

She pretended to think about it, taking her time to look around the living room too. It had more than its share of windows, and the bright sunshine made the room look spacious and inviting.

"This place *is* nice. . . . And a month isn't really *that* long." A month was a *very* long time. Surely within a month she would be able to break down Liam's resistance. Surely, after even just a few more days of living in the same condo, she would be able to convince him to give in to the desire she now knew he was burying deep inside.

But as if he could somehow read her mind, Liam shook his head. "I don't know. Maybe we should keep looking."

That would be okay too. She shrugged. "If you think that's best."

"On the other hand, we might never find another place this nice."

Marisala crossed her arms and leaned against the wall. "This really shouldn't be my decision," she told him. "I would have been happy to live in more than half of the apartments you vetoed."

Liam laughed ruefully. "Yeah, I know. *I'm* the head-case. But it *should* be your decision, Mara. What do *you* want to do? Just because *I* like this place doesn't mean you have to like it too."

If she had her choice, she'd prefer living in a busy house filled with roommates. Like Dan's. Or like

Liam's, especially now that Inez and Hector were around.

"Can you handle having me live in your place for an entire month?"

He hesitated only very slightly. "Yeah," he said. "I can handle it."

Marisala gazed into his eyes, marveling at the way he could keep all of his emotions, all of his doubts and fears and desires safely hidden from her.

"Okay," she said, turning to the landlord. "I'll take it."

She'd take it, and pray that a month really *was* enough time. One thing was for certain: October first was further away than September first—the date by which she'd expected to move out of Liam's house. And she also knew that the longer she stayed with him, the better her chances were of getting under his skin.

And maybe, just maybe, a little bit into his heart.

SIX

Liam was back in the prison. It was dark, he could barely see, but he recognized the overpowering smell and the pervasive dampness.

Confusion nearly knocked him over. No, he couldn't be back here. This couldn't be real. *Could* it?

It was a dream. Wasn't it?

Or maybe the sunshine and fresh air were the dream. Maybe delirium had brought vivid images of life back in Boston—Marisala with him in Boston. How unlikely was *that*? Maybe he'd never gotten free. Maybe . . .

He stumbled, realizing he was being led upstairs, hands tied securely behind his back. His wrists were raw and his back burned from his most recent beating.

He was going to be beaten again. They never brought him up from his cell for any other reason.

At least he would be outside. The chance to breathe fresh air was almost worth the beatings.

He held his head high as he was led past the captain

of the guards, pushing his mouth up into a smile. It always ticked off the guards when he smiled at them.

He'd learned to smile even as the whip cut into his back.

But this time the captain smiled back. "You've had a visitor. A girl was so eager to find you, she broke into the compound."

A *girl*. Marisala. Fear rose in his throat, threatening to choke him. He worked to hide it, knowing he couldn't give away the fact that she was important to him. Still, he had to ask, "Where is she?"

The captain smiled again. "I'm afraid she did not survive her altercation with the guards."

He saw it then. A body. *Her* body, crumpled lifelessly in the dirt. Long, dark, bloodied hair kept him from seeing her face, but still he knew. It was Marisala. It had to be.

"No!" He broke free from the guards and ran toward her. He could hear their laughter as they chased him, as they easily brought him down, face-first into the dust.

He was barely a yard away from her, but he still couldn't see her face. "No!"

They dragged him away, laughing and kicking him as he shouted his anger. He had to see her face. He had to know.

And then the wind lifted her hair, and he *could* see.

Marisala's face, caught in a grimace of death, eyes gazing unseeingly toward the sky—

❖━━━━❖

Liam bolted upright in his bed, his heart pounding, his breath catching ragged and thick in his throat.

A dream. It was just a dream. Marisala was alive and safe and sleeping two doors down from him.

Or was she? His clock radio said it was nearly eleven A.M. Dammit to hell, he'd slept through Marisala's first morning of classes.

Closing his eyes, still trying to slow his heart, he forced himself to think clearly, slowly. Maybe sleeping through this morning had been for the best. After all, what had he thought he was going to do? Go to class with her? As much as he wanted to tag along, he knew that was the last thing she wanted.

There was really only one place that Marisala wanted his company, and that was in bed.

She must've made three trips down to the kitchen last night after she'd put on her nightshirt. He'd been in the living room, trying to read the latest file on the state sex-offenders registry that Lauren Stuart had given him when he'd stopped by her apartment earlier in the evening.

When Liam had turned away to keep from being distracted by the sight of Marisala's long legs, she had come into the room to ask him a question. Something trivial. If she didn't get back in time for lunch tomorrow, would he please walk the puppy?

With her recently brushed hair down and glistening around her shoulders, dressed in an oversized T-shirt that clung to her body, revealing it in brief, tantalizing flashes, with her long, slender, gracefully shaped legs, she was hard enough to resist. But it was the look in her eyes and her smile of awareness that nearly pushed him over the edge.

She was *trying* to drive him insane.

And she was banking on the fact that she could succeed and end up in his bed before she moved out on October first.

God, how had he gotten himself into this mess?

What on earth had possessed him to agree that she stay with him for an entire *month*?

He wanted her. There was no denying that a very major part of him wanted nothing more than to throw this girl down and lose himself in her sweet fire.

But he was more than a man with an erection. He was a man who had learned exactly what he could and could not live without. And while he knew he could live—albeit painfully—without Marisala in his bed, he wasn't sure he could live without her friendship.

He swung his legs over the side of the bed. His head was pounding and his mouth tasted like hell. He pulled on the shorts he'd worn yesterday and staggered toward the kitchen and the smell of brewing coffee.

As Liam went in, Hector was cutting vegetables at the counter.

It was strange how much he liked having other people living in his house. He liked waking up to the sound of someone working in his kitchen. God knows he had enough money, he should have thought of hiring kitchen staff years ago.

"How's Inez today?"

The puppy jumped at the sound of his voice and ran a quick circle of joy around Liam before returning her attention to her rawhide toy. She looked clean, her fur coat shiny. Marisala no doubt had managed to give her a bath last night while he was out picking up that file from Lauren.

"Inez is feeling poorly, señor. She is lying down." The man at the counter was the same height and build as Hector. He also had the same heavy accent as Hector. But when he turned around, he wasn't Hector at all. He was a stranger—a much older man, with streaks of gray in his hair and years of wisdom in his dark eyes. "I will be helping her in the kitchen today."

"Ah," Liam said, reaching to get a mug from the cabinet. "And you would be? . . ."

"Ricardo Montoya." The man bowed very slightly, a smile softening his craggy facial features. "It is a great honor to meet you, Señor Bartlett. You have done much for my country."

Liam poured himself a cup of coffee. "So, where exactly did Marisala find *you*?"

"At the Boston Refugee Assistance Center," Ricardo told him. "Downtown. Marisala came by early this morning. I was delighted to see her. We fought together in San Salustiano."

Liam sat down at the table. "So, naturally, she invited you to come live here." He knew this was going to happen. Marisala was going to collect strays until every bedroom in this house was filled.

Amusement twinkled in the older man's dark brown eyes. "No, señor. She asked me to come and stay with Inez today. Hector was offered a one-day job with a landscaping company in Brookline that he felt he couldn't turn down. But he was unhappy at the thought of leaving Inez alone all day with the baby due any moment. And Marisala has classes until eleven."

"I was here—she should have just woken me up."

"She told me she couldn't bring herself to wake you." Ricardo turned back to his onion. "She knows too well how elusive sleep can be. I, myself, still have trouble at night, and I only spent two months in the prison. You, señor, were there much longer. Nearly eighteen months, no?"

The prison. Images of his dream flashed through Liam's head, suffocating him. God, this was the last thing he wanted to talk about. "I don't remember, exactly. I lost track of the days. . . ."

Ricardo moved to the sink and quickly washed several stalks of celery, shaking them dry and carrying them back to the cutting board. "It was hard to keep track of the days and the nights—it was dark most of the time," he said. "I remember thinking it was like being buried alive—"

Liam stood up, trying to shake off the sound and image of his cell door swinging shut with an ironlike clank. He didn't want to think about it. He *couldn't* think about it. He turned away. "I better get busy if I want to shower before Marisala gets home," he said briskly.

"The scars on the back, they fade, señor. But the ones on the soul, they fester unless they're tended." Ricardo smiled gently as Liam turned back to stare at him. "And although you walk around, coming and going as you please, if your soul is still locked in the darkness, you are not truly free."

Understanding hit. "You *work* for the Refugee Center, don't you?"

Ricardo smiled again. "Yes, señor. That I do."

"And when you introduced yourself to me, you left out a little detail, like the word *doctor* that comes before Montoya. Doctor—as in psychologist, am I right?"

Ricardo shrugged as he serenely returned to his chopping. "It is merely a label. Unimportant. First and foremost, I am a man—one who has known a bit of the hell you once knew."

"Marisala asked you to come here not to baby-sit Inez, but to baby-sit *me*. She thinks just because I have an aversion to basements, I need—"

The phone rang, interrupting him.

Even Ricardo stopped cutting, pausing to wait and listen as the answering machine picked up.

"Hector calls in every hour to check on Inez," he explained over the sound of Liam's voice telling the caller to leave a message at the beep. "Don't worry, señor—I will not pick it up unless I am certain it is him."

The machine beeped and an unfamiliar voice came on the line. "Hi, yeah, this is Dan Griswold calling for Marisala—you know, from the house on Commonwealth Avenue in Allston?"

Dan. It was Dan of the goatee beard and the too friendly smile. Liam sighed in exasperation.

"I got your message, and I'm sorry that you're not interested in being one of our housemates, but I understand about your uncle's friend being a little uptight."

God, what had Marisala told him? Her *uncle's* friend?

"Even though we're not going to be housemates, I hope we can be friends," Dan continued. "I, uh, I wanted to invite you to a party we're having over here on Saturday night, around eight. You don't need to call me back—unless you, um, need a ride or something. Anyway, I hope to see you then. Bye."

Liam cursed under his breath. Something about Dan pushed every single one of his buttons. Especially when he called to ask Marisala out on a date.

Ricardo had returned to chopping peppers, but after the machine clicked off, after several moments of silence, he spoke. "Men are drawn to her. Despite all that she's been through, she has a sweetness most men find hard to resist." He glanced at Liam and smiled. "You should resign yourself to receiving many more of these phone calls. Or prepare to . . . what is the American expression? Stake your claim."

Liam turned abruptly toward the door. He didn't want to talk about *this* either. "Right. I'll be in the shower."

The puppy perked up her ears and barked, then dashed into the entryway, nearly knocking Liam over in his haste to reach the front door as Marisala pushed it open.

"Well, hello," she said to the little dog, kneeling down to greet her. "Hello, Evita. Don't you look beautiful today. Now, wasn't that bath worth it?"

She looked up to see Liam and blushed. He knew it wasn't his lack of shirt that embarrassed her, but rather the fact that he'd caught her giving the puppy a name.

"You've named the dog *Evita*?" He couldn't help but laugh.

She laughed, too, even as she lifted her chin defensively. "I couldn't just keep calling her 'puppy.' Besides, her owners haven't called about her yet."

"They will."

"Not necessarily."

"Mara, don't let your expectations get too high." Liam was talking about more than the puppy, and they both knew it.

She gazed up at him. "You must've met Ricardo."

"Yes, I certainly have met the good doctor. He tried to give me therapy with my coffee. I, however, prefer my coffee black."

"You always were too smart for your own good." Holding Liam's gaze, Marisala called down the hallway, " *'Dias, Rico.*"

"*Buenos dias, Marisalita,*" the other man called back. "Lunch will be ready in thirty minutes."

Liam lowered his voice. "If I want therapy, I'll find myself a doctor on my own. Am I making myself clear?"

She didn't even blink. "I thought it would help if you knew there was someone you could talk to. Someone who had actually been in the prison—"

He changed the subject. Pointedly. "I'm sorry I wasn't awake to see you off this morning. You should have gotten me up."

She gave Evita's floppy ears one more rub then straightened up. "I couldn't. I went into your room, but . . . you looked so peaceful. Did you sleep well?"

The picture from his dream—her body crumpled in

the dirt of the San Salustiano prison—crashed into his mind, pushing aside the provocative image of her in his room, watching him as he lay asleep in his bed. He carefully kept his voice even. "I slept. How were your classes?"

Marisala snorted. "Ridiculous."

"In what way?"

"In *every* way. The topics. The professors. The other students. It was worthless."

Liam sat down on the stairs and took a sip of his coffee. "What happened? Something must've happened, because that sounds like a classic Marisala knee-jerk reaction to me."

"*Nothing* happened. It was awful. I had two classes this morning—"

"American history and English lit. I know."

"The history lecture was absurd. There were so many people in the lecture hall, I could barely see the professor from where I was sitting. He spoke in a monotone! I would have learned more from reading a book. And the literature course! We're starting by reading a book about a dog." She glanced down at the puppy. "No offense, Evita dearest, but I'm sitting there, thinking why am I here? Why am I going to read a book about a *dog* when there's so much else I could be learning? And the literature discussion group was stupid. I'm in a group with six other students—six *children*—and all they wanted to talk about was the party at the Student Union last night."

Liam took another long sip of his coffee.

"I *hated* it," Marisala said flatly.

He couldn't hide his smile. "Yeah, I . . . um, kind of got that impression."

"It's *not* funny! What am I going to do? If I have to sit there," she fumed, "*wasting* my time—"

"Maybe you should think about changing your major."

"To what? I've already looked through the course catalog, and I didn't see any listings for classes in strategic warfare. That's the only thing I'm good at!" Marisala pushed her way past him up the stairs, the puppy on her heels.

Liam followed too. "Maybe you *should* think about joining the army, getting into some kind of officers' program—"

She laughed, but it sounded brittle as she pushed open the door to her room. "Oh, *that* would be perfect. All those years I spent fighting, living for the day I could *stop* fighting. And now you think maybe I should spend the rest of my life fighting?"

She sat down on the bed, her shoulders slumped in dejection. "What am I doing here? I should have just married Enrique and gotten it over with."

Liam stopped in the doorway, knowing it would be a mistake to get too close to her. But he wanted to. God, he wanted to put his arms around her. He held his coffee mug more tightly instead.

"How do you stand it?" she asked quietly. "How do you walk around and still manage to smile?"

She looked up at him, and her eyes were fiercely intense. "During the history lecture, I was sitting next to a girl who just broke her fingernail. She acted as if it were the end of the world. She actually left the lecture to find a nail file. And I was sitting there thinking, is this real? Is this what real people worry about? Broken fingernails. And parking spots? On my way to class, I saw two men nearly come to blows because they both wanted the same parking spot." She shook her head. "I wanted to slap them and make them see how petty their problems are." Her voice shook. "I wanted to give them a list of all the children I knew who died in that war I was so good at fighting."

Liam knew she was close to tears. "Please, just go away," she told him. "Just close the door and leave me alone."

He knew he should. He knew that was *exactly* what he should do. Close the door and walk away.

Instead, he stepped into her room. Instead, he set his mug of cooling coffee on her bedside table. Instead, he sat down next to her on the bed and took her hand, gently lacing their fingers together.

"We'll figure this out," he said, wishing he felt as confident as he sounded. "I know a guy, he's a career counselor—he's got this standardized test that you fill out, and it tells you what kind of job you're most suited for. I'll help you, Mara, and together we'll find some classes that'll interest you."

She glanced at him and smiled, but turned away before he got a clear look at the tear that had escaped from the corner of her eye. As she furtively wiped it away he pretended not to notice. God, when was the last time he'd seen Marisala cry?

"You're going to help me, huh?" Marisala took a

deep breath and forced another shaky smile. "You, the king of the maladjusted?"

"Ouch—*that* hurt."

She laughed, and Liam lost himself for a moment in the bottomless depth of her eyes. As he watched, an awareness dawned in those eyes, an awareness and a haunting vulnerability.

She wanted him to kiss her, her body language couldn't have been more obvious. She wanted him to kiss her, but she didn't expect him to.

She looked away, but then glanced back. She had something to ask, and in true Marisala style, she took the bull by the horns. "Do you find that my scar makes me terribly ugly?"

Of all the things Liam had expected her to say, *that* wasn't one of them. For a moment he was speechless. *Ugly?*

"I think Santiago wanted me to go to a plastic surgeon because he doesn't like looking at it," she continued. "I think he doesn't like being reminded of the war."

Liam couldn't help himself. He touched the side of her face, tracing the crescent shape of her scar with his thumb. "It's not ugly," he said. "But when I see it, my knees feel weak, because I can't help but think how close you came to being killed."

"So it does bother you."

He lifted her chin so she was forced to meet his gaze. "Do *my* scars bother you?"

To his surprise, tears once again filled her eyes, and

she nodded. "Yes," she whispered. "More than you can possibly know."

She touched him then, turning his shoulder so that she could see his back. He knew it didn't look pretty. It was covered with a latticework of fading scars, handiwork of many lashings from a lifetime ago.

He pulled away from her. "I'm sorry. I'll make sure I wear a shirt from now on."

"No," she said. "That won't make them go away. It'll only *hide* them. You don't really think that just because something is covered up, I'll forget that it's there?"

The tears in her eyes overflowed, spilling down onto her cheeks.

When her father and her brother died—that was the last time Liam had seen Marisala cry.

She tried to stop, tried to push her tears away, but she couldn't.

And in the same way, Liam couldn't keep himself from reaching for her.

She fell into his arms as if he were her safe harbor. She clung to him, her arms tightly around his neck, her face buried against his throat.

And Liam knew that coming here to Boston was much more difficult for Marisala than she had let on.

He knew that the war had killed the innocent young girl both he and Santiago remembered. Despite Santiago's wishes, there was nothing any of them could do to get that little girl back.

And Liam knew that whatever he did—whether he rejected Marisala for the sake of their friendship or he gave in to this burning need to make love to her—it didn't matter.

Whatever he did, it would only make her feel worse.

He could only hope that, in the long run, keeping his distance would hurt her less.

SEVEN

Marisala looked out of the window as Liam slipped the car into a parking spot. As usual, one had magically opened up for him as he pulled onto the busy downtown street. He was inordinately lucky, but only when it came to finding places to park. The rest of his life wasn't quite as charmed.

She'd woken up in the night again to the sound of him caught in a nightmare. She almost went into his room, but then his light went on. From her doorway, she could see him through the crack in his slightly open door. As she watched he rushed toward her and flung the door open wide.

She swiftly and silently moved back into the shadows of her room as, breathing hard, Liam flung himself at the light switch in the hall. The light came on, glaring and bright, but even that didn't seem to be enough for him. As she continued to watch he went downstairs, dressed only in his boxer shorts, and turned on every lamp in the house—with the exception of the ones in her room and in Hector and Inez's.

When she saw Liam this morning, it was obvious that he'd been up for the rest of the night.

He hadn't had a good night's sleep in a week—not since that morning she'd first gone to her classes and he'd slept until nearly noon. Maybe it was time to call Ricardo Montoya again. But the last time they'd talked, her old friend had pointed out that he couldn't *force* Liam to talk to him.

And God only knew *she* couldn't force Liam to talk to *her*.

He hadn't even told her where they were going this morning until she was in the car.

Of course, he'd been right about one thing—if he *had* told her where they were going, she probably wouldn't have gotten into the car. Because they were going shopping. He was taking her shopping for clothes.

Marisala climbed out of the car as Liam put coins in the parking meter. "I don't need new clothes. I like the clothes I have."

"Two or three outfits," Liam said firmly. "That's all we need to get. Just enough for you to wear when Santiago comes to visit."

"If he's not coming until Thanksgiving, why do we need to shop *now*?"

Liam held open the door to one of the fancy stores that lined the street. "Because you have to get used to wearing them."

Marisala stopped short. "Oh, no. No way—"

"You don't have to wear them all the time. Just every

now and then. As a matter of fact, there's a charity ball
I've got to attend next week. It's a good opportunity for
you to—"

"You're not making me go to a *ball*!"

Liam closed the door, resigned to standing out on
the sidewalk and discussing this. "I thought all females
liked balls—like you all have some kind of Cinderella
gene."

"I got a Rambo gene instead. I'll skip the ball, thank
you."

"Mara, you've got to practice all this social-etiquette
stuff I've been telling you about."

"At a *ball*? I don't think so."

"If you can handle that, you can handle Santiago."

"I can practice keeping my mouth shut anywhere.
That's what it all boils down to, isn't it?"

"It's more than that, and you know it. You need to
wait and watch and pick up signals from other people.
You need to let them take the lead. If you're at all uncertain as to how formal or casual to be, let them set the
pace and the tone. If you wait for them, you can pick up
cues. We've talked about this—"

"Endlessly," she said dryly.

"This would be a great opportunity to try it out on
strangers—"

"No," Marisala said. "Read my lips. No. No, I'm
not going to a ball."

"Don't decide now. Think about it."

She paused for a half a second. "I've thought about
it. No."

"It could be fun."

She laughed. "Yeah, right."

Liam gestured toward the door. "Come on. We can do this quickly and get it over with, or we can take forever and really suffer."

Marisala went inside. "There's just one problem," she said as he closed the door behind them. "You didn't mention we were going shopping until after I was in the car."

"So?"

She leaned closer and lowered her voice. "So I'm not wearing any underwear."

The look on his face made her wish she'd brought her camera.

The situation wasn't quite as awful as she made it sound. It wasn't as if she simply had neglected to put her underwear on this morning when she got dressed. In fact, the running shorts she wore were the kind that had a panty built right in. As for a bra, she didn't have the type of body that needed a great deal of restraining, and she only wore one underneath her T-shirt when she ran.

Or when she knew she was going shopping for clothes.

Liam took a deep breath, and Marisala knew that he was determined to pretend he wasn't fazed by her announcement. "So?" he said. "Big deal." He pulled a dress from the rack. "What size are you?"

"Not *that* size," she said, making a face at the big red-and-purple flower print of the dress. "Believe me. They don't make *that* dress in *my* size."

Liam pulled another from the rack. "How about this?"

It was better. It still had a floral print—most of the clothes in this store did—but the flowers were tiny and the swirls of blues and greens were actually pleasant to look at. "The skirt's too long. I'll trip over it when I run."

"Ten-to-one odds are you won't be running while you're wearing this," Liam pointed out. "I'm guessing you're a small." He took another dress from the rack, and another.

Marisala sighed. "I suppose the next stop is the hairdresser's."

"Nope—just the drugstore to buy you a hairbrush. You have beautiful hair. It would be a crime to cut it." He thrust the load of dresses into her arms. "Try these on."

She gasped. "Liam! Did you look at these price tags? One of these dresses would feed a family of eight in San Salustiano for an entire week! I couldn't possibly buy this—it's insanely expensive."

"Just try it on."

"I will *not*!" Marisala flung the dresses onto one of the racks and headed toward the door.

Liam smiled. Perfect. She'd done exactly what he'd expected her to do. He followed her out onto the sidewalk. "You want to come back inside and try that again?"

This was to be another of their lessons in civility. They would go back into the store, and maybe this time she would finally learn how to talk politely, to stay calm, to curb her passionate nature.

There was genuine surprise in her eyes. "Excuse me?"

"Obviously you haven't listened to a single word I've told you about how to deal with people like Santiago. If I were your uncle, I'd be pretty disgusted with you right now."

"But—"

"If you don't like that store, if you don't like those clothes or those prices—that's fine. But come on, Mara, you've got to learn to drop the high drama. Turning your back and walking away . . . That was rude."

"Rude?" Two circles of pink appeared on her cheeks. "*Rude?* What's *rude* is that price tag on that dress! No, it's not rude, it's *obscene*! How could you take me to a store like that? How could you think I would wear a dress like that when people are going hungry? Even here in this country, people are hungry! I see them on the streets all the time!"

"So *talk* to me about it. Don't shout at me. Come on, let's go back into the store and do this over, without any shouting."

She laughed in disbelief. "I will *not*. Some things need to be shouted about, and this is one of them!"

"There's a time and a place for shouting," he told her, trying to keep his own voice calm.

"Yes, and it's *all* the time and *every*where," she countered.

"It can be possible to make a stronger statement with a softer, more rational voice. You need to learn to recognize when shouting will be useless. It's useless with Santiago—you know damn well he can outshout you any day. And it's useless with me. All you need to do is talk, even quietly, and I'll listen to you."

"But I *like* to shout—and believe me, I'll shout some more if you make me go back into that store!"

His voice got louder despite his best efforts. "Marisala, you're being difficult on purpose. You know exactly what I'm trying to do."

"Yes, I do. You're trying to show me how to stay silent when my heart wants to cry out. You're trying to teach me to smile when I want to weep. You're trying to make me hide all that I feel, to never let it show—to be like *you*." There was real contempt in her voice. "The only time you shout about anything is in your sleep."

Liam couldn't respond. What could he possibly say?

She stalked toward his car. "Take me to a store with lower prices, and I'll show you all I've learned so far about your way of hiding."

Liam unlocked and opened the car door, knowing better than to hold it open for her. He got in behind the wheel and headed toward a low-priced department store.

Some things need to be shouted about. The only time you shout is in your sleep.

She was right. Dear God, she was absolutely right.

He couldn't remember the last time he'd shouted in anger instead of fear.

"Hector did *what*?" Marisala's new sandals skidded on the kitchen floor, and if it weren't for Liam's strong arms, she would have landed directly on Evita. But he quickly released her as if touching her burned him.

"Hector got a job," Liam answered for Inez. "That Brookline landscaper hired him."

"Full-time," Inez added, lowering herself uncomfortably onto one of the kitchen chairs.

Marisala let out a whoop. "That's fabulous!"

Liam was grinning. "Yeah, isn't it?"

There were tears in Inez's eyes. "He wouldn't have gotten the job if he didn't have an address and a phone number to give the supervisor. If you hadn't helped us . . ." She smiled tremulously. "We were so lucky."

As Marisala watched, Liam tried to lighten the solemnness caused by Inez's touching gratitude. "Well, we were lucky too. I mean, think about it. Marisala could very well have brought home someone who would think nothing of murdering us in our sleep."

"That wouldn't have been a very big problem for *you*," Marisala countered, "seeing as how you never sleep."

Liam crouched down to scratch behind Evita's floppy ears. "And *you*, of course, have your ferocious watchdog to keep you safe."

Inez was giggling instead of weeping—exactly what Liam had intended. "You two look so nice all dressed up in your fancy clothes."

Marisala held out the long skirt of her dress so that Inez could see. "Fourteen ninety-five—can you believe it? Pretty good deal, huh?"

"What do you think, Evita?" Liam asked the puppy. "Do you want to make a bet whether or not Marisala can refrain from telling the waiters and the busboys at the restaurant how much her dress cost? You think she can? *I* think she can't. *I* think she's going to stand up on the table and make an announcement about it to everyone in the entire restaurant."

Marisala squinted at him in her best version of her Great-Aunt Selena's evil eye. "You don't believe I can go out to dinner with you and 'behave,' as you call it."

"I'll believe it when I see it. And of course, it's not like going to that charity ball. But we've already established that you can't handle *that*."

"I won't have to go to a ball with Santiago when he visits. Going to dinner is *much* more similar to—"

"It doesn't matter anyway," he teased. "I don't think you'd be able to find an evening gown for under twenty bucks."

"Aren't you embarrassed by the fact that the tie you're wearing cost nearly *four times* more than my dress?"

"I think she's going to make that announcement at the restaurant as well," Liam told the puppy.

"Four *times*," Marisala repeated. "Doesn't that make you feel decadent and evil?"

"Yeah, yeah, right. Decadent and evil. My two middle names." Liam gave Evita one more scratch behind the ears and straightened up. "Let's get going, shall we?"

"Give Hector a big kiss for me when he gets out of the shower," Marisala told Inez.

Inez smiled shyly. "I will."

"And tell him not to cook tonight," Liam added.

"I'm going to have the restaurant send your dinner over. You and Hector deserve to celebrate too."

The tears were back. "Thank you so much."

Even Marisala looked a little misty-eyed. "Oh, Liam, you're so sweet."

"I thought I was decadent and evil."

"Decadent, evil, *and* sweet. What more could I possibly want in a dinner date?"

"This isn't a date," he protested. "It's another of our lessons."

Marisala smiled angelically as she swept out the door. "Good. Maybe this time you'll finally learn a thing or two."

"Are you familiar with the expression *rule of thumb*?" The light from the candle played expressively across Marisala's face as she gazed across the table at Liam.

"Of course," Liam said. "It means something that's standard. Something everybody knows."

He let himself gaze at her—after all, it would have been rude not to. They were having dinner. They were in the middle of a conversation—a civil one, no less— and it made perfect sense for him to look at her.

Good thing, because he wasn't convinced he'd be able to keep his eyes off her if it were otherwise.

"Do you know where that expression comes from?" she asked.

It was amazing how incredible she looked dressed in a little cotton nothing of a dress. The miniature flower print and the cornflower-blue color were pleasant enough, but it was the dignity with which she wore it that commanded the attention.

And she *was* getting a boatload of attention. The waiters and the maître d' of this little Italian restaurant had been hovering ever since they'd arrived.

With her hair down, curling around bare arms and shoulders that were exposed by the sleeveless cut of the dress, and with a touch of the makeup he'd bought for her, she was, hands down, the most beautiful woman in the room—quite possibly in the world.

The tiny tattoo of a flame on her left arm only made her seem more exotic.

She was watching him, one eyebrow raised slightly, waiting for him to answer her question.

Liam had to search his memory to remember exactly what that question was.

Rule of thumb. She had just asked him a question about the expression *rule of thumb*. "Is it some kind of measurement thing?" he guessed. "As in the average man's thumb is a certain number of inches long?"

He'd toyed with the idea of taking her to one of the fancier restaurants farther downtown—one of the ones that had no prices on their menus. But all that would've gotten him was another argument, not dinner.

"Well, there are some people who believe that the expression comes from woodworkers who used the length of their thumbs to make measurements, but there are others who think the expression comes not from the length of a man's thumb but the *width*. Some people think the original rule of thumb was from an old church law in which a man was allowed to beat his wife with a stick as long as that stick was no thicker in diameter than his thumb."

Liam nearly choked on his wine. "You're kidding!"

Marisala shook her head. "There are similar laws in San Salustiano pertaining to . . . domestic discipline, shall we call it."

"God, I didn't know that."

"In San Salustiano, when a man marries, his wife becomes his possession. If she works, her paycheck is often addressed to him. Women are allowed to vote, but most women don't even go to polls. There are loophole laws, which allow a man to vote for his wife, provided she is unable to leave her home due to sickness." She laughed in disgust. "It's amazing in San Salustiano how many women are suddenly bedridden on election day."

She took a deep breath. "In some villages, women are not allowed to speak in church. Women are strongly discouraged not to run for office. They *are*, however, expected to work slave hours for slave wages, and then come home and care for and cook for and clean for their husbands and families."

"No wonder you don't want to get married."

Marisala smiled, but it didn't touch her eyes. "I would have married for love, but not for money."

"You must've . . ." Liam cleared his throat. "Did you love Enrique very much?"

She took a sip of her own wine and shrugged. "I don't know. I thought I did at the time. Now I'm not so sure. The sex was great, though."

Liam refused to let her see the effect her casually tossed-off words had on him. Still, he couldn't think of a single thing to say in response to that statement. *The sex was great.* Dear God. He knew without a doubt that making love to Marisala would be an experience unlike any he'd ever had. All that untamed passion and energy . . . The sex would be *beyond* great.

Thankfully, she changed the subject. "Oh, I meant to tell you. Today I received the results from that test I took—you know, that career counselor's test?"

"You actually took it?" He was genuinely surprised. "You filled it out and sent it in and . . . everything?"

"Of course I did. You asked me to." She smiled. "You'll never guess the career that most accurately fits my background and personality."

Liam had to smile, too. "I'm afraid to."

"Smart man. I'll give you a hint. It wasn't a homemaker, that much is for sure. Come on. Guess."

"Longshoreman?"

Marisala laughed, a musical explosion of delight, and three waiters immediately approached to see if she needed more wine. She waited until they refilled her glass, and thanked them before turning back to Liam. "That was very close," she told him, her eyes still laughing. "But not close enough. That test of yours revealed that I would be happiest and most successful as a construction foreman. Or as a political lobbyist. Either one." She rested her chin in the palm of her hand as she gazed across the table at him. "Can you believe it?"

"Well, okay. So seeking help from a questionnaire didn't work. It was worth a try, though." Liam took another sip of wine, thinking hard. "Have you thought about law enforcement?"

"If I never hold another gun in my life, that would be too soon for me. If you want to know the truth, I'd rather be a construction foreman. I'd rather spend the rest of my life building things—giving life instead of taking it away." She rolled her eyes. "Besides, how well do *you* think a female cop would go over in San Salustiano."

"Maybe," Liam said carefully, "you should think about staying her in Boston. If things are so bad there for women, maybe you shouldn't go back."

Her dark eyes were bottomless as she gazed at him. "San Salustiano is my home," she finally said. "I would need a very powerful reason to keep me from returning to my home."

"How about the fact that in San Salustiano, women are second-class citizens? Isn't that powerful enough?"

"That doesn't make me want to stay away," Marisala told him. "It makes me want to go back to try to change things."

"I thought you'd had enough of fighting."

"As long as I don't have to use a gun, I'll be happy to fight."

"Okay, so maybe that political-lobbyist suggestion wasn't too far off the mark. Maybe what you need to be doing is taking courses in poli sci. Or law. Maybe you should think about going to law school."

"That's what Dan's been telling me."

Liam froze. "Dan."

"You know. From the house on Commonwealth Avenue. He works as a teaching assistant in the history department. I've run into him a few times on campus."

He swore. "I bet he's made sure of that."

Marisala bristled. "And what is *that* supposed to mean?"

Liam couldn't hide his frustration. "Oh, come on, Mara. It's obvious what the guy wants, isn't it?"

For a moment he thought she was going to raise her voice and lash out at him. But instead of getting louder, she got very quiet. "Actually, yes," she said. "It *is* obvious. Dan likes me exactly the way I am. He doesn't want me to change the way I act or walk or talk. He likes me. He likes *me*—not some revised version of me, redesigned according to Santiago's and your precise specifications. He doesn't need me to wear fancy clothes—"

"He doesn't want you to wear *any* clothes."

Her temper finally flashed and she slapped the tabletop with the palm of her hand. "You've met the man exactly once! How can you be so sure—"

Liam looked at his watch. "Not bad. You managed to keep in control for ninety-seven minutes. You're going to have to do a little bit better, though, when Santiago comes to visit."

Marisala laughed in disbelief. "You're kidding, right? You *baited* me! Santiago's not likely to attack me with that stupid, macho jealous crap of yours! In fact, I'm willing to bet Santiago will *like* Dan!"

She was right. Liam knew she was right. "Let's just change the subject, all right? Do you want dessert?"

She stood up. "No, I do not want dessert. Nor do I think we should change the subject. The fact is, Liam, you don't want me, but you don't want anyone else to have me either."

"That's not true." He'd gone too far. Talking about Dan had pushed him over the edge, but now it was too late to do more than deny her words. He *did* want her. He wanted her desperately. He knew she would misinterpret his denial, but he couldn't tell her the truth. He wasn't even sure anymore what the truth was.

"If that's not true, then you won't mind if I head over to that party at Dan's house? The party you never bothered to give me the phone message about?"

Liam's stomach dropped. Dan's party. He'd honestly forgotten. "God, I'm sorry—"

"You can't have it both ways, Liam." She gathered up the backpack she used for a purse, slipping the strap over her shoulder. "You've decided you don't want me. That means you have to stop acting like a jealous lover and let me live my own life."

"Mara, please sit down and—"

"Thank you for dinner. Most of it was lovely. I'll see you after the party."

EIGHT

He was in the jungle.

Hiding.

The night was dark and misty. Moisture dripped down from the trees, further obsuring what little vision Liam had.

A platoon of government soldiers were mere yards from the spot he and Marisala had dug into to spend the night. She was still sleeping, still exhausted from the fever that had kept her out of the action these past four days running. He could hear her quiet breathing as she lay in her damp bedroll on the rain-soaked ground. Dear God, he had to get her to shelter or she'd never get well.

Liam's own barely healed wounds ached and throbbed, but he forced his thoughts away from his own discomfort.

He could smell the cigarette smoke that clung to the soldiers' breath and clothing. Under Marisala's leadership, the guerrillas had learned to give up smoking. They'd learned the lingering odor of cigarette smoke was a dead giveaway when hiding in the underbrush. It was a *very* dead giveaway, in the most literal sense of the word.

One of the searching soldiers moved closer, and Liam flattened himself against the ground, trying to become one with the earth.

But then, beside him, Marisala stirred.

"Liam?" A whisper of breath, then louder, a trace of panic in her voice as she sat up. "Liam!"

The soldier hadn't heard or seen her—yet. Liam knew, though, that if Marisala called out for him any louder, she'd be heard.

He moved. Swiftly. Silently.

He pulled her back down, covering her mouth with his hand and her body with his.

"Be quiet," he breathed into her ear. "Soldiers at ten o'clock. Quiet!"

She struggled beneath him. No doubt the fever was making her delirious. He held her tighter, willing her not to give them away.

Her hair smelled sweet and fresh, fragrant from a recent washing and . . .

A recent washing?

Liam opened his eyes.

Brightness streamed through his open door and across his bed, illuminating Marisala.

He was lying on top of her, his hand securely clamped over her mouth. She bit his hand, and he pulled it back. "Ouch!"

She was breathing hard. "Liam, this is *definitely* not the time for you to lose it! There're no soldiers in this room. Just me and you. Come on! Are you back here with me? I need you back here with me."

He wasn't in the jungle. He was . . . somewhere warm and dry. He was in a bed. Lying on top of Marisala.

"We're in *Boston*," she continued.

"Boston," he said. It didn't make sense. Why were they in Boston? Her hair smelled so clean and sweet. He wanted to bury his face in it, to pull her even closer. "But I was . . ."

"You were dreaming," she told him.

Dreaming. The jungle was only a dream. Instead, he was here with Marisala, in his bed.

God, what was she doing in his bed? She fit beneath him so perfectly, so familiarly, an incredible blend of soft flesh and supple muscle. Their legs were intertwined, his thigh pushed up tightly between hers. He felt his body respond and knew she couldn't help but feel it too.

When had they become lovers?

But wait, her clothes were on. She was still wearing a dress he recognized from . . . dinner? Yes, she'd worn that dress to dinner. They'd had dinner together tonight, out at a restaurant that was both miles and years away from that island jungle.

"Inez is in labor," Marisala told him. "And as cozy as it is lying here with you like this, we've got to get her to the hospital *now*. The baby's coming *fast*."

Inez. Labor. The baby . . . Liam rolled off Marisala

as reality and his memory came crashing down around him. He and Marisala *weren't* lovers. He was her guardian, for God's sake.

His boxer shorts did little to conceal his body's immediate response to finding her in his bed and Liam tumbled onto the floor in a hasty attempt to cover himself.

His hands closed around denim and he wrestled with his jeans, yanking them up his legs as Marisala pushed herself off his bed and headed toward the door.

She hesitated in the doorway, looking back at him. "Are you sure you're okay to drive?"

"Yeah, I was just . . . I'm just . . . Yeah, I'm awake now," he told her as he struggled with his zipper and searched for his sneakers and T-shirt. "How was . . . how was the party?" How was Dan? he wanted to ask.

"It was fun. Dan was very glad to see me."

Liam tried to bite back his response but couldn't. "I bet."

"I'll be in the kitchen with Inez and Hector." Marisala headed down the stairs. "Hurry."

It was too late.

One look at Inez, and Marisala knew the baby was coming now.

Liam came into the kitchen, car keys in his hand, hopping on one foot as he slipped his other into a sneaker. His hair was charmingly disheveled, and his chin glistened with golden-brown stubble. "Which hospital?" he asked, raking his hair back out of his eyes. "Does it matter?"

"We're not going to make it to the hospital," Marisala told him, quickly rolling up her sleeves and washing her hands in the kitchen sink. "Call an ambulance, see if we can get a doctor or paramedic over here pronto. Hector, get some clean towels and sheets, and bring them into your bedroom. Inez, come with me."

Liam was stunned. "We're not . . . going to? . . ."

From upstairs, from where she'd locked the puppy in her bedroom, she could hear Evita whimpering.

"Liam, please call 911." Marisala kept her voice calm, afraid of frightening Inez as she led her into the back bedroom. "This baby is not going to wait."

"I want to push," Inez sobbed in her native Spanish, gripping Marisala's arms.

"That's so good," Marisala told her, helping the younger woman up and onto the big double bed, and into a crouching position. "That means it's almost over. You're doing fine. This is just the way God intended it to be. Everything is happening exactly as it should."

Hector was backing out of the room.

"Hector, help your wife," she commanded him in that same gentle voice. She arranged the towels underneath Inez, twisting to get a good look at the top of the baby's dark head. A few more minutes and the worst would be over.

Hector looked as if he wanted to run away. "But . . ."

"Isn't this your baby?" she asked him, her words

gentle but her gaze hard as stone. "Didn't you have something to do with the conception? Now it's time for you to help with the slightly more challenging part, don't you think?"

"Paramedics are on their way." Liam was standing in the doorway. "They should be here in about ten minutes."

Marisala met his eyes. He knew as well as she did that ten minutes would be too late. This baby was coming *now.*

"Have you done this before?" His voice sounded breathless.

"Yes, I have." Marisala helped hold Inez up between contractions. She smoothed back the younger woman's hair as Liam watched, murmuring words of encouragement. "Many times. We didn't have access to many doctors during the war, so many of us learned enough to take their place when necessary." She smiled wryly. "It was often necessary."

Liam found it difficult to think of Marisala as anything more than a mere girl. She dressed like a girl. She spoke with a young girl's often tactless honesty. But how many girls knew how to deliver a baby? How many girls could take instant and absolute command of a situation like this?

His breath caught in his throat as he watched her. She was so gentle with Inez, yet so strong. She was exactly what Inez needed. And Inez clung to her, holding her gaze with complete faith and trust in her eyes.

"You're doing fine," Marisala told the younger woman, her voice soothing. "In just a short time this will all be over. In just a short time you'll hold your son or daughter in your arms, and you'll know that this will have been well worth it."

Inez nodded.

"Talk to her," Marisala urged Hector, who was looking a little green. "Tell her you love her. Tell her how wonderful and brave she is. Tell her how sweet it's going to be, to hold that little baby of yours."

The sound of Hector's soft Spanish hummed in the background as Liam took a deep breath. "What can I do to help?"

Marisala smiled at him, and he saw that she had tears in her eyes. "Wash your hands, and then come help me hold Inez."

He hesitated. "Shouldn't she be lying down?"

"Only if she wants to fight gravity. This is the way women were meant to give birth. But this position makes it a little more difficult for the doctor. That's why most Western women have to give birth upward—kind of like launching a rocket—for the doctor's sake. In my experience, this position is far more pleasant for mother and child. Please go wash your hands."

Inez tensed and moaned, and Hector went another shade paler.

"Breathe," Marisala commanded them both. "Keep breathing!"

Liam ran to the kitchen sink and quickly scrubbed.

There was a crash from the other room and the sound of Marisala biting off a curse. "Liam, I need your help!"

He ran back, drying his hands as he went. Hector

was out for the count, facedown on the bedroom floor, and Marisala was trying both to hold Inez and deliver the baby.

Inez clung to her and Marisala couldn't break free. "Support the baby's head," she commanded Liam.

"Me!"

Inez shrieked as another contraction gripped her.

"Do it!" Marisala shouted, and Liam lunged forward, twisting to reach underneath Inez, watching in horrified awe as more and more and still even more of the baby's head appeared like some kind of monster trying to break free.

He could hear Marisala helping Inez to push, helping her bear down, crying out with her, turning Inez's sobs into shouts of triumph.

And then, all in one squishy, amazing, incredibly miraculous movement, the baby's head slid into his waiting hands. A face—a tiny, red, scrunched-up, impossibly ugly, blood-and-fluid-covered face—was pressed against his palms. It was unbelievable.

"Breathe," he heard Marisala say, and he drew in a breath along with Inez. Dear God, it was unreal, and yet more real than anything he'd experienced in years.

"One more big one," Marisala told Inez. "We're almost done!"

Inez groaned, and the baby was pushed into his hands. It moved, quivering and trembling, and Liam struggled to hold on, terrified he'd drop it, shifting it into his arms, blood and all. The umbilical cord draped over his arm, still connecting the baby to his mother.

"My God, it's a boy," he breathed.

It *was* a boy. A tiny, slimy, red-faced, newborn boy. An innocent child, with his entire life stretching out before him—a life filled with hope and promise and endless possibilities.

The baby drew a deep, shuddering breath and let out a loud, mewing cry.

The sound of a newborn baby's cry still haunted his dreams, but he couldn't think about that now—he wouldn't think about it.

"One more push," Liam heard Marisala tell Inez, her voice thick with emotion. "One more for the afterbirth, and then you can hold your son."

Inez was crying, but her tears were not from pain. Her pain had faded almost instantly at the sight of her baby. As Marisala helped settle her back on the bed, she stretched out her arms, and Liam carefully handed her the infant.

Hector was back. He'd struggled to his feet, his face still an odd shade of green. He valiantly tried to ignore the blood and fluid that drenched the sheet and towels. He kissed his wife and they gazed raptly together at their child, as if that screaming, scrawny, mottled red thing in Inez's arms was the most beautiful sight in the world.

And it was.

Liam had never seen anything more perfectly beautiful.

The doorbell buzzed, loud and long, as if someone were leaning on the button.

"The paramedics," Mara murmured. "Good. Just in time to tie off the cord."

Liam didn't want to leave. He didn't want strangers coming in and taking Inez and the baby away. He wanted to hold that baby again, to look down into that little boy's swollen face, to welcome him more completely to the planet Earth. He wanted to hang on to this sense of peace, this feeling of hope. God, it had been so long. . . .

But the buzzer rang again, and Liam wiped his hands on a towel as he went to answer the door.

He led the paramedics—a man and a woman—inside, and he stood in the doorway, no longer needed, as they helped Marisala cut the cord and wrap the baby in a clean towel.

Marisala came toward him then, exhausted and triumphant. Her new dress was stained. It was ruined, but she was smiling. Liam had never seen her look so radiant. "You were wonderful," she said.

"*I* was? God, *you* were. That was . . . it was . . ." He shook his head. Dear God, he was on the verge of breaking down and sobbing like a baby himself. He had to blink hard to keep back the tears that were welling in his eyes.

"They've named him William," she told him, blinking back her own tears. "After you."

Liam laughed—afraid if he didn't do something he'd burst out crying. "Me? Why me?"

Marisala took his hand. "Because if it wasn't for your generosity, that little baby might've been born on the street. If it weren't for you, he would've been born homeless."

Liam shook his head. "It wasn't me. It was *you*. You brought them here. You gave them a place to stay and a way to save their pride. I did nothing."

She laughed. "Nothing? You've shown them respect and kindness. You treated them like human beings."

"I only followed your lead. They should name the baby after you."

Marisala touched his face. "They know where you've been," she told him quietly. "They've already chosen to name their child after a man who is both kind *and* brave."

"I've done nothing," Liam said again. "Even in prison—I simply endured."

The sound she made was somewhere between laughter and a sob. "But you *did* endure, and every day I thank God."

She turned away, wiping her eyes as the paramedics prepared to take both Inez and the baby to the hospital, to be checked by a doctor.

Liam knew for a fact that he'd done nothing, except learn to hide. He'd done nothing, except forget that there were things in life that needed to be shouted about. He'd done nothing but try his best to stop living that life that had stretched out before him so pristine and filled with hope on the day he'd been born.

He'd done nothing, because even though his body was free, he'd left his soul still locked in the darkness of that prison cell.

Marisala heard the unmistakable sounds of Liam's nightmare. A strangled cry, a flurry of motion, and then lights.

All over the house, she heard him turn the lights on.

The clock on her bedside table said it was 3:54.

It had only been a little more than an hour since Hector had gone with Inez to the hospital. It had only been an hour since she'd fallen thankfully into bed and closed her eyes.

She heard the sound of Liam on the stairs, heading back to his room, and she swung her legs out of bed. She crossed to her door, opening it wide.

He saw the movement and turned to look at her. He looked exhausted, but she knew he wasn't going to sleep anymore tonight.

"I didn't mean to wake you," he said quietly.

He was wearing only his boxer shorts, and despite the hum of the central air-conditioning, his body was slick with sweat, his hair damp and sticking to his face and neck.

"You didn't," she lied. "I was awake—I couldn't sleep."

He didn't buy it for one second. "Yeah, right."

She came out into the hall. "Bad dream?"

There was heat in his gaze that he tried to hide as he looked away from her. "Just go back to bed."

"I could do that," she said. "Or . . . as long as we're both awake, we could talk."

He sat down, right there on the stairs, as if his legs could no longer hold him up. "I'm not sure I know how to talk anymore." He glanced up at her. "You know, about things that are important."

Marisala held her breath, amazed that he'd said even *that* much.

He laughed, and when he spoke again, his voice sounded bitter. "I've become a pro at small talk, though. I don't suppose you want to talk about the weather. . . ."

She sat down next to him. "What do *you* want to talk about?"

He turned slightly to face her. "You're good, aren't you? I mean, in dealing with people. You have an excellent bedside manner."

Marisala wasn't sure she understood. "Is that good or bad?"

"It's good. I was thinking . . . it occurred to me tonight that you should go to medical school. You should be a doctor, Mara."

She laughed in surprise. "A *doctor*? Be serious."

He smiled back at her, and there was actually a trace of his old sparkle in his eyes. "I am. Dead serious, my friend. You'd be a fabulous doctor. You could specialize in obstetrics. You know, delivering babies. Helping create instead of destroy."

A *doctor*. She'd never considered that. But during the war she *had* spent as many hours tending the wounded in the hospitals as she'd spent on the front lines. "As a doctor in San Salustiano, I wouldn't be able to just deliver babies," she said, thinking aloud. Mother of God, was she actually considering this? "There's a serious shortage of general practitioners."

He leaned forward, his eyes a blaze of blue intensity. "I'll help you apply to medical school."

"I'd have to take classes for *years*."

"It'll be very hard work, long hours . . . but I know you could do it, no sweat."

She looked up at him again. "Santiago won't approve."

"I'll talk to him. He'll be fine. I promise."

Marisala believed him. If anyone could handle Santiago, it was Liam. Liam could charm anyone, he could handle *any* situation. Or so she'd once believed. "I'll think about it." She changed the subject abruptly. "So what were you dreaming about?"

He was silent for a moment, just looking at her. The sparkle left his eyes and once again he looked almost ill with fatigue. He was silent for so long, she was certain he wasn't going to answer. But then he did.

"The baby," he finally said. "I was dreaming about the baby."

Marisala frowned. "Inez and Hector's?"

"No."

Silence stretched on and on, until Marisala couldn't stand it any longer. "Tell me," she whispered. "Why won't you tell me?"

"Because it was terrible," he said quietly, and she saw that there were tears in his eyes. "Because I keep hoping if I don't talk about it, if I don't *think* about it, maybe it'll go away."

He sat in silence for a moment, his forehead resting in the palm of his hand, his elbow on his knee. When he looked up at her, his eyes were rimmed with red, but he still fought back his tears. Marisala wondered if he ever let himself cry.

"It's not working," he finally admitted. "I haven't forgotten any of it. It's always back there, waiting for me to fall asleep. All those memories. They're not just going to go away, are they?"

She shook her head no.

"Yeah, I didn't think so."

He reached for her, holding out his hand for hers, and she took it, lacing their fingers together. She had to fight her own tears as she held tightly to his hand, as she prayed he would reach out for her again, this time with words.

One minute stretched into two, two into three, and still she waited.

When he finally spoke, his voice was barely audible.

"A pregnant woman was brought to the prison," he told her. "I don't know what she did, what she was being held for—she didn't know herself. She was put in the cell next to mine. I didn't know her that well—she was only there for a few days, but . . ."

He stopped talking, and Marisala realized he was struggling to keep from crying. She wished he would just let go, that he would allow himself the emotional release. The Liam she'd known in the jungle all those years ago would've let himself cry. But this man had learned since then to keep everything inside. This man had learned to hide everything he felt—even from himself.

"There was a vent that connected our cells, it was barely an inch wide, but I could hear her, and she could hear me. We talked at night when the guards were asleep.

"Then one day she was taken up top, and I was so afraid, because I knew they were going to beat her." His voice broke. "How could they beat a pregnant woman?"

He gripped her hand even tighter.

"But they did. They whipped her. And when they threw her back into her cell, she told them she was injured. I heard her tell them that her labor had started, that she needed medical help, but the guards just laughed and locked the door. She gave birth to her baby alone in that cell. And then she died. She bled to death, Mara. God, they just let her die."

Liam let go of her hand and pulled her close, burying his face in her hair. He was crying. He was finally crying, but Marisala felt no satisfaction. Mother of God, maybe she had been wrong. Maybe it was better for him to try to forget all that he'd endured at the hands of the monsters who had imprisoned him.

But his story wasn't over. "She knew she was dying. She called to me to help her, to save the life of her baby. She begged me, but what could I do? I shouted myself hoarse, calling for the guards. I could do nothing—except listen to her die."

Marisala held him closer, weeping along with him, wishing she had the power to take away his pain.

"And then," he told her, "after she was dead, I heard the baby crying. For nearly eighteen hours I could hear her baby cry."

"I'm sorry," Marisala said. "I'm so sorry."

"While I was listening to that baby cry, I thought

that it was as bad as any of the tortures I'd endured. It was awful, Mara. But then . . . Then it got worse." He had to take a breath. "Because then, the baby stopped crying. And then, I had to face that terrible silence."

He was quiet then, just holding on to her. Marisala was quiet too. There was nothing she could say.

"How do I live with that?" Liam asked brokenly. "How do I live with that memory? With that—and all the others?"

"I don't know," she admitted.

"I came home from that hell. I walked away, and I thought I was finally all right. I thought I could leave it all behind. But I can't forget. I try, but I can't."

Marisala could feel his scarred back beneath her fingers. She wanted nothing more than to help him, but she couldn't. There was nothing she could do.

Or was there? Maybe she *could* help him to forget— if only for just a little while.

She turned her face toward him, feeling the rasp of his beard against her cheek. She brushed her lips across his, tasting the salt of his tears. She felt him pull back, but when she kissed him again, he didn't move quite as far out of range.

He did protest, though. "Mara, no—"

She silenced him with another kiss, and with another, and another. And then, with a volcanic rush of need, he kissed her, claiming her mouth almost savagely, pulling her toward him.

His hands slipped up and under the edge of her nightshirt as he crushed her to him, as he swept his tongue into her mouth, as he kissed her harder, deeper.

She felt a flash of giddy disbelief. He wanted her. He was finally acknowledging that he wanted her as much as she wanted him.

The sensation of his hands against her bare back was exquisite as he kissed her again and again, deep, dizzying kisses that consumed her and burned her to her very soul. She could feel his arousal and she straddled his lap, pressing herself against him, wishing for nothing between them—no T-shirt, no boxer shorts, and especially no doubts.

She heard him groan as his hand cupped her breast, and she pulled slightly back and drew her shirt over her head in one swift motion.

"Mara, we shouldn't," he protested, even as he touched her, even as he buried his face in the softness of her body, as he drew first one nipple and then the other into his mouth. The sensation was incredible, and Marisala cried out.

This was what she had dreamed of for so long. Making love with Liam. There was no should or shouldn't. There was only need. She shifted her hips, covering him more completely, feeling him strain against her.

She was on fire and she saw answering flames in his eyes.

"Come to my bed," she whispered.

He wanted to. She knew he did. He was touching her hair, running his fingers across her breasts and her back, tracing the outline of the tiny flame tattooed on her arm, filling his hands with her as if simply looking wasn't enough.

He met her gaze, and she could see him give in to

his desire. He stood, picking her up with him, and started up the stairs.

And then the telephone rang.

The answering machine picked it up after only one ring, as it always did. Liam paused, and from down in the kitchen, they could hear the sound of his recorded voice, telling the caller to leave a message after the beep.

"I am sorry to be calling so late at night—or early in the morning, depending on your perspective, I suppose." Santiago. That was Santiago's voice.

Liam stiffened, and the look in his eyes was that of a little boy caught with his hand in the cookie jar. "God, how did he know?"

"I wanted to call to tell you that I am all right," Santiago continued. "You probably haven't even heard the news, but there was a fire earlier tonight at the capitol building."

A *fire.* Marisala slid down from Liam's arms. On her way down the stairs she grabbed her shirt and slipped it on.

"President Estes was injured," Santiago was saying as she hurried into the kitchen. "I, too, was taken to the hospital, but all I suffered was a little smoke inhalation. I didn't want you to hear the reports and think I was in any danger."

Marisala picked up the phone. "Hello? Santiago?"

"I'm sorry, Marisalita, did I wake you?"

"No. I was . . . We were . . ." She turned to see Liam standing in the kitchen door, watching her, his expression wary, as if he expected her to tell her uncle exactly what they had been doing. What they had been about to do. What she hoped they would still do, after she got off the phone. "We were awake," she said, turning away from Liam's distracting blue eyes to give her uncle her full attention. "We were . . . talking. Are you really all right?"

"I am." She could hear relief in his voice. "Felipe Estes was also lucky. We've just had word he's going to be all right."

"Who set the fire?" she asked fiercely. "Who was responsible for such a terrible thing?"

Santiago laughed. "You're not going to believe this after all the violence our country has been through, but the fire was the result of a power surge during an electrical storm."

"Are you sure?"

"Quite positive. I myself saw the lightning strike."

"Thank you so much for calling. If I'd heard the news on CNN without knowing—"

'I know," he said quietly. "Is Liam close at hand? May I speak to him?"

"Yes, he's . . ." But Liam was no longer standing in the doorway. "He *was* here. I'll go get him—"

"No, don't trouble him. It's late. No doubt you've worn him out with your . . . talking."

Was it her imagination or had he really put an infinitesimal and innuendo-loaded pause into that sentence? Marisala felt her cheeks heat with a blush. Did her uncle guess that the conversation she and Liam had been having had not been one with spoken words?

She had to say something, so she blurted out the first

words that came to mind. "Santiago, I'm considering going to medical school to become a doctor."

He was silent, but not for long as she'd expected. "What does Liam have to say about that?"

"It was his idea."

"Have him call me. We will talk when it's not the middle of the night. Good-bye, Marisala."

As she hung up the phone she turned to see Liam standing once again in the doorway. But unlike before, he was now fully dressed. He'd put on his jeans, a polo shirt, and his sneakers, and he held his car keys in his hand.

Marisala couldn't hide her disappointment. "I was hoping you'd gone upstairs to take your clothes off, not put more on."

"Mara, I can't stay here tonight. If I do, you know what will happen. You know where this thing between us will go."

She held his gaze. "I for one would like very much to go there. I think I've made that absolutely clear."

Liam had to look away. He couldn't believe he was having this conversation. He couldn't believe he was about to walk out of his house instead of taking this beautiful, dynamic, sexy-as-sin woman up to his bed.

"You have," he said carefully, not sure what to say to make her understand. Their relationship was too precious for him to risk ruining it forever. Just because he wanted her more than he'd ever wanted any other woman in his life didn't give him that right. "And if I didn't care so much about our friendship, and about my friendship with Santiago—"

A combative glint appeared in her eyes. "This is between us. Santiago has nothing to do with this."

"Santiago has *every*thing to do with this. Santiago is the reason you're here in Boston," Liam countered.

"I want to make love to you," Marisala said. "There. I've finally said the words." She crossed her arms in front of her, taking a deep breath. "I won't tell Santiago if you don't."

He ran his hand through his hair in frustration. "Mara, this isn't some game—to tell or not tell. Okay. Forget about Santiago. Let's pretend he *hasn't* asked me to be your guardian. Let's pretend you're right and he has nothing to do with us. Still, this is about you and me. This will change everything between us—forever. If we sleep together, there's no going back."

"Sleep together." She rolled her eyes. "You're hiding again, this time behind euphemisms. Sleep together—it sounds so safe, so antiseptic. But we've slept together in the same tent many times, and I know that's not what you mean. You mean if we let ourselves give in to desire. You mean, if you dare to fill me with your passion, if we make hot, sweaty, raw, ecstasy-filled, pulse-pounding physical *love*—"

"Yes." Liam needed her to stop. God knows he was strong, but he wasn't *this* strong. "Yes, that's exactly what I mean. If we . . . do that . . . If we become lovers—"

She was standing in front of him, wearing only her nightshirt and a pair of panties. The thin cotton clung to her body revealingly, but even if it hadn't, he *still* wouldn't have been able to shake the image of her, in his arms, wearing almost nothing at all.

"What if it's *incredible*?" she implored him. "What if it's *perfect*?"

How could making love to Marisala be anything *but* perfect? The way she'd felt in his arms, the euphoria he'd felt kissing her . . . He'd been caught off guard, he'd been unbalanced, his resolve weakened, and if that phone hadn't rung, he would be in Marisala's bed right now, driving himself hard and deep inside of her again and again until she cried out and . . .

But the phone *did* ring, and sanity had returned, and with it had come the bitter truth.

He was in love with this girl. Christ, he had been for *years*.

He didn't want a night or two of mindless passion. He didn't want hot, sweaty, raw, ecstasy-filled, pulse-pounding physical love—as she'd said. He wanted Marisala's heart. He wanted her soul. He wanted to give her his own heart and soul in return.

But he couldn't do that until he knew for certain that someday, and someday soon, his soul would be his own again to give her.

"I'm not ready for something perfect." His quiet words must've rung true, because she stopped her assault. She looked away from him, and he knew she didn't understand.

All she understood was that he was turning her down. He was rejecting her. Again.

"You don't have to leave your house," she said softly. He followed her gaze out the kitchen window and he saw that the sun was coming up, filling the eastern sky with the promise of morning.

"I have some things I have to do," he told her. He had to find Ricardo Montoya at the Refugee Center. He had to call Santiago. He had to make damned sure he was doing this right.

And doing this right meant that he had to let her believe—at least for a little while—that he didn't truly want her. Because if he let her know the truth, if she realized just how hot he was for her, and more important, just how much he cared, she wouldn't let up until they were naked together in his bed.

"I'll see you later," Liam told her as he headed for the door.

He didn't look back.

He didn't dare.

NINE

Liam's car was parked in front of the building.

Marisala saw it as soon as she turned the corner and started down the block.

Evita wanted to stop and sniff the newspaper box, but Marisala tugged on the leash, urging the puppy to break into a run.

Liam was finally home.

In fact, he was coming out of the building, carrying some kind of garment bag over one shoulder, holding open the door and—

He wasn't alone. He was with a woman. He was with a very tall, very blonde, and very elegant woman, whose silk shirt and suit jacket were the polar opposite of Marisala's ragged cutoffs and tank top.

Marisala knew the moment Liam saw her. He damn near flinched, as if seeing her and being reminded how close they'd come to making love last night was painful to him.

Still, he greeted her politely. "Mara. I figured you were out walking Evita."

The blonde laughed. "The puppy's name is Evita?" She held out her hand to Marisala. "You must be Marisala. I'm Lauren Stuart. It's so nice finally to meet you."

Lauren Stuart of the husky-voiced phone calls. Marisala felt her stomach drop down to her toes. Lauren was beautiful and poised, with carefully coiffed hair and perfect fingernails. Surely she was jealous of Marisala living in Liam's house, but her words didn't reveal even the slightest negative emotion.

There was no doubt about it. Even if Lauren wasn't Liam's lover, she was everything Marisala was not. It was little wonder he kept pushing Marisala away.

"We've got an awards luncheon to go to," Liam told her. "And the annual Fund-raisers' Ball is tonight, re-member? The award ceremony could go on all after-noon, so I figured I'd better pick up my tuxedo so I could go to the ball directly."

So he wouldn't have to come home to change. So he wouldn't have to be alone with her. Marisala couldn't fight the rush of disappointment and hurt that swept over her. So instead, she made like Liam, and smiled, hiding it. "Yes, of course, I remember."

"I won't be home until late." Liam unlocked the passenger door of his car and held it open for Lauren. "Don't wait up for me."

"Nice to meet you, Marisala." Lauren settled grace-fully in Liam's car with a sensuous whisper of silk.

"Have a good time tonight," Marisala told the other woman, nearly choking on the words.

"Oh, I'm not going to that fun fest, thank God." The blonde smiled. "I'm heading out to San Francisco this afternoon. My sister's getting married tomorrow, bless her perfect timing." With another smile, she closed the car door.

Lauren wasn't going. Which meant that Liam would be there alone . . .

He stood looking at her across the top of his car. He looked wiped out, exhausted. "Have you spoken to Inez or Hector? When I called the hospital, there was no answer."

"I talked to Inez about an hour ago. She was very tired—she might've unplugged the phone. But both she and the baby are doing fine."

Liam nodded. "Good." He hesitated, lingering as if he had something else to say. "I did a little research on the university's pre-med program. It's too late to do anything about this semester, but you can apply for January. I mean, if you don't want to go somewhere else . . ."

"Dan's stepfather is on staff at the medical school at New York University. He thought it would be easier to get into the program with some kind of connection like that."

Liam's expression didn't change. "You spoke to Dan."

"I saw him over at school this morning. We had coffee after class."

There was a sudden flash of jealousy in his eyes that

he couldn't hide. "Don't tell me—he's graduating law school this year, after which he intends to get a job in New York City, right? Dammit, this guy is about the *least* subtle—"

"Don't start with that again," Marisala hissed. "You have no right—no claim on me. And Dan is my friend. He likes me. And if you think anything you say will make me stay away from him, then you need to have your head examined!"

She turned to storm inside, but he stopped her.

"Mara."

She turned back, but kept her eyes firmly on the street. She didn't want him to see the hurt that lurked behind her anger. How *dare* he have the gall to act jealous with Lauren Stuart sitting right there in his car?

His voice cracked. "I'm sorry and . . . I have. Had my head examined. At least I've started to. It takes a while, you know?"

Marisala couldn't believe what she'd just heard. She looked up at him. "What are you saying?"

He smiled crookedly. "I'm saying that I spoke to Ricardo Montoya this morning. There's a Thursday-night group that he runs—all people who were in San Salustiano during the war, believe it or not. I'm going to try going. See if it . . . helps. You know."

Marisala *did* know. She knew exactly what he'd done, and exactly the courage it had taken to do it. She picked up Evita and hugged the puppy to keep from throwing herself over the top of the car and into Liam's arms. "That's good," she whispered.

"I was hoping . . ." He faltered.

"I'll come with you. If you want," she quickly added.

"I'd like that. But . . . think about it first. You might find it pretty intense—you were there too. I don't want you walking into the fires of hell with me, so to speak, without considering the implications first."

"Fires don't scare me." She managed to smile at him. "And we've already been to hell and back, you and me. . . ."

He nodded. "I've got to go."

"We can talk later," she agreed.

"Tomorrow," he said. "Don't wait up for me tonight."

"I won't." She wouldn't wait. Because she was going to see him before that. Lauren Stuart or no Lauren Stuart, Marisala was going to this charity ball.

Because she now knew with a terrifying conviction that she was, without a doubt, completely in love with this man.

She was going to prove to Liam that she'd been paying attention to all those lessons on how to talk and walk and act in polite company. She was going to show him she could be everything he wanted in a woman, and more. She was going to make him forget about Lauren Stuart and convince him that tonight was a perfect night to take their friendship one step further and become lovers.

She wasn't looking for anything permanent. Neither of them was. They'd both learned too well that nothing lasted forever.

But she was willing to take whatever time he could give her—whether it was a year, a week, or even just a few hours. She loved him enough to risk everything for a chance to be his lover, even just for one night.

As Liam pulled away, Marisala headed back toward the funky shops on Newbury Street. She was going shopping.

"May I get you another drink, sir?"

Liam gazed pensively down at the ice cubes in the glass in his hand, but shook his head. "No, thanks. I'm fine." He was so tired, the single gin and tonic he'd already had was making his head buzz. If he had any more, he'd have to take a cab home.

He glanced at his watch, moving off to the side of the ballroom, wondering how long he'd have to stay before he could duck out and head for home. Ten o'clock. Surely he'd be able to go home at ten.

Marisala was at home.

The image of her straddling his lap, kissing him, her bare breasts peaked tightly beneath his hands, brought heat and a solid heaviness to his body. Perfect. Nothing like having an erection the size of the John Hancock Building to really make his evening complete.

He moved closer to the wall, hoping none of the society ladies who had set up this bash would spot him and pull him onto the dance floor. He closed his eyes, letting the music wash over him, praying for ten o'clock to arrive so that he could leave.

He'd told Marisala not to wait up for him, but he had no doubt that waiting up for him was exactly what she was doing. He would go home, he would unlock the door, and he would find her curled up in a chair in the living room, completely naked, reading a book. She would look up at him and smile and . . .

"There you are. I've been looking all over for you."

Liam opened his eyes and nearly fell over.

Marisala wasn't at home. She was standing directly in front of him, fully dressed.

She looked incredible. Her hair was down, framing her face. She had on more makeup than he'd ever seen her wear, and it polished her wild beauty, making her look older, more elegant and refined. Her dress was simple—a plain, black, sleeveless sheath that hugged her curves and ended many, many inches above her knees. She wore high-heeled sandals on her feet and sheer stockings on her legs. Liam wasn't sure he'd ever seen her wear stockings before. In fact, he was certain he hadn't.

"What are you doing here?" he asked stupidly.

"My Cinderella gene must've kicked in. I had an uncontrollable urge to come to the ball."

He was staring at her—he couldn't help himself. "God, you look beautiful."

"Thank you." She smiled. "I'm here to practice being good. So I'll only tell you how much this dress cost if you ask."

Liam had to laugh. "Oh, yeah? What if I don't ask?"

"Then you'll never know that I picked it up at a thrift shop for only nineteen dollars."

Liam felt his heart expanding so that it filled his entire chest. He felt light, almost giddy. He felt every cell in his body come alive as he let himself drown in

Marisala's laughing eyes. "Dance with me." It wasn't a request, it was a command, but she acquiesced prettily, lowering her eyes almost shyly.

She let him take her hand, let him lead her onto the dance floor.

Liam smiled as he took her into his arms. "Boy, I'm glad you came."

She gazed up into his eyes. "I am too."

He had to keep talking, because if he wasn't using his mouth to talk, he was going to use it to kiss her. "I went to the hospital after the luncheon, but Inez was still sleeping."

She moved closer, slipping her hand up onto the back of his neck and gently resting her cheek against his. Her skin was so smooth, so soft. His pulse began beating in uneven triplets.

"Hector was there." He cleared his throat, but he couldn't get rid of the huskiness. "He must've just come from work—his hair was still wet from his shower. He was just standing there, watching both Inez and his baby sleep. I don't think I've ever seen a man look so happy and proud."

She smelled so good. Liam wondered if she could feel his heart pounding. He knew she could feel his body's undeniable response to her as she moved even closer.

She was so beautiful. He could see people watching them, wondering who she was. He could feel the buzzing interest of the men in the room—it was almost a palpable thing. Marisala seemed oblivious, though. Her full attention was on him.

"I've spoken to both Inez and Hector." Her breath was warm against his ear. "If they haven't found a place to live that they can afford by October first, I've told them that they can temporarily move in with me."

October first. It was only a few weeks away, and those weeks were shrinking fast with every day that passed. On October first, Marisala would move out of his place and into her own apartment. He would be alone again.

Liam didn't want to think about it, didn't want to talk about it, so he did the only thing he could.

He kissed her.

She melted against him, parting her sweet lips and letting him greedily drink her in. He could taste her answering passion and her triumph, and he knew this was what she wanted. She'd come here tonight to seduce him, to conquer the last of his resistance.

He was thoroughly seduced and more than ready to surrender. He had been from the moment he'd opened his eyes to find her standing in front of him. He had been from the moment he'd left his apartment this morning to find her standing on the sidewalk, next to his car.

"I want to take you home," he murmured, pressing her even closer to him, making certain she knew how much he wanted her. "I want to take off your clothes and make love to you."

Her voice was husky too. "Isn't this where you say 'but' and tell me a thousand reasons why we can't do that?"

"No buts this time. I can't fight this anymore. You

win." He laughed. "In some ways, I guess I win too." He kissed her again, sweetly, slowly—a promise of the pleasure-filled night to come. He felt her catch her breath, felt her tremble in his arms. "I spoke to Santiago today."

Her eyes were wide as she pulled back to look at him.

"I told him that I couldn't be your guardian any longer. He guessed the reason why."

Somehow Santiago had known that he and Marisala were on the verge of becoming lovers. He had seemed pleased about it, even when Liam had rejected his offer.

"Did he . . ." She had trouble saying it, and had to take a breath and start again. "Did he try to talk you into? . . . "

"Yeah." Liam nodded. "He offered me a rather substantial dowry to marry you."

Marisala closed her eyes. "Oh, no."

"I turned him down. I told him I didn't need his money." He took her hand and pulled her off the dance floor. "Come on, let's get out of here."

The relief that flooded through her was laced with an odd disappointment. But what had she thought? That Liam would want to *marry* her? Surely she knew better than that. Besides, she wasn't interested in marriage.

Once outside of the ballroom, they went down the stairs to the hotel lobby much too slowly. Marisala forced herself to hang back, to let Liam lead. He'd told her that often enough—to keep from coming on too strong even in a conversation, let the other person lead. Let them set the pace and tone.

Liam looked impossibly handsome dressed in his tuxedo. The jacket and pants were tailored to fit him perfectly, and the black color made his golden hair gleam in contrast. His eyes had never looked so blue.

He led her across the ritzy hotel lobby at a pace that nearly made her scream with frustration. She wanted to get home now. Sooner than now! She wanted to run to his car and pull out of the parking lot with squealing tires. She wanted . . .

Before they reached the doors, Liam took a quick turn and drew her with him off to the side onto a small balcony. No one else was there, and he pulled her into his arms and kissed her.

His kisses were in direct contrast to his seemingly easygoing pace. They were possessive and fierce, leaving her breathless and desperate for more.

"I want to throw you over my shoulder and run all the way home," he whispered, "but if I do, everyone will know why we're leaving so early."

"I think they probably know anyway," she told him. There was not a single woman in that hotel who hadn't given Liam a second glance and Marisala an envious look.

Liam tilted her chin, studying her upturned face in the dim light as he led her back into the lobby and out the main doors onto the sidewalk. "God, I knew you were pretty, but when you go all out, you're . . . Mara, forget about medical school. You could make a fortune as a fashion model."

"Ah, just what the women of San Salustiano need—a fashion model to lead them in their fight for equal rights."

He laughed. "Good point. But, you know you can't live your entire life for other people. You have to do some things simply because *you* want to do them." He started down the sidewalk. "I'm parked about a block down—right on the street."

"I do plenty of things for myself," she countered. "Right now, for instance, I'm going home to do something entirely for myself." She smiled. "With your help, of course. And you *do* get some fringe benefits."

He pulled her into his arms and kissed her again, right there on the street, next to his car. He kissed her inside the car, and at every stoplight they hit. The rest of the time he drove with his foot on the floor, pushing the speed limit as high as he dared, finally moving at a pace that didn't drive Marisala crazy.

And then at last they were home, racing together up the stairs, fumbling with the key in the lock. But once inside, Liam didn't throw Marisala over his shoulder and carry her up to his bedroom, the way she'd expected. Instead, he went into the kitchen and took a bottle of champagne from the refrigerator. As she watched he took two delicate flutes from the cabinet.

"Let's go in the living room," he said.

Marisala didn't want to go into the living room. She wanted to go upstairs. She was done with waiting. She wanted Liam *now*. But again, she gave in, aware of her resolve to let him lead, afraid of ruining this new image she'd created by suddenly coming on too strong.

She followed him into the other room and watched as he set the bottle and the glasses down on the coffee table. He turned on only one light and it cast a golden glow over the room, warming the comfortable furnishings. He sat down on the couch and smiled up at her.

Marisala slowly sat next to him as he began wrestling the cork free from the wine bottle.

"I bought this to have when Hector and Inez bring the baby home from the hospital," he said. "But I'll pick up another bottle, because we've got to have champagne tonight."

The cork popped with a rush of foam, and laughing, Liam filled both glasses. He handed one to Marisala. "Here's to an unforgettable evening."

He clinked his glass against hers, holding her gaze as they both took a sip.

Marisala felt her heart do a slow flip as he smiled at her again. He was unbelievably romantic, but she didn't want romance. She didn't want anticipation. She wanted him.

Liam set his glass down on the table, then took her glass and did the same. Marisala knew with a rush of fiery heat that this was it. He was going to make love to her now.

But instead of rising to his feet to lead her upstairs, Liam dropped to his knees. He took her hand, bringing it to his lips and lightly kissing her palm, her wrist.

"Marry me."

At first she didn't understand, didn't grasp what he was saying. His words didn't make sense.

"You have to marry me," he told her, his eyes as

intense as his voice. "Marisala, I don't want you just for tonight. I want you forever."

She stared at him in total shock. Liam Bartlett was on his knees before her, proposing marriage. But Mother of God, she didn't want to *marry* him! She didn't want to marry *any*body. He wasn't supposed to want her this way. She'd never dreamed he'd want more than a love affair.

"But . . . what about Lauren Stuart?" She knew it was a stupid thing to ask, but she couldn't help herself.

He stared at her, confused, but it didn't take him long to make the connection. "You thought? . . . " He laughed. "No, Mara, Stuart and I are just friends. We've never been anything but friends. She's my boss. Did you really think? . . . "

"I asked if you were sleeping with her, but you wouldn't tell me. So I assumed you were, and then when I met her . . ."

"You were wrong."

"I'm glad." She was. She was more glad than she wanted to be.

"Look, I'm not perfect," he continued. "You know that probably better than anybody. I've got a lot of stuff to work out. I haven't written a word in months. I've got to figure out what I'm going to do with my life if I can't write anymore. Hell, maybe I'll go to medical school with you." He smiled. "Maybe I'll train to become your nurse."

Marisala had to laugh at that. "Liam . . ." She shook her head.

"Don't say Liam, just say yes."

He was watching her, waiting with such expectation and anticipation for something she couldn't possibly give him. She didn't know what to say, didn't know what to do, so she slid down off the couch onto her knees on the floor next to him and she kissed him. "Liam, make love to me."

He nodded. "I suppose after 'yes,' that's the next best thing you could've said."

"I want you so badly," she whispered. "I want to feel you inside of me."

He laughed, and when he spoke, his voice cracked expressively. "Yeah, that was effective too."

She kissed him again, and this time he kissed her back with delicious abandon, his hands sweeping her body as possessively as his tongue claimed her mouth.

His fingers found the back zipper of her dress as she pushed his jacket off his shoulders. Marisala knew he felt a similar frantic need to rid them of their clothes, but also like her, he couldn't stop his kisses.

His arm got stuck in the sleeve and he laughed in frustration, taking a moment to pull it off of him, turning the jacket nearly totally inside out in his haste.

Marisala wriggled out of her dress and kicked off her sandals, laughing at the volcanic flare of heat in his eyes as he saw her underwear. It was black and sheer and it had cost far more than the dress she'd worn over it. There were some things that were worth spending money on. There would only be one first time with Liam. God, when she'd bought the undergarments this afternoon, she'd thought there was a real possibility there'd be only one time with Liam, period.

But now he'd gone and mentioned the F-word. Forever.

With a sudden shock, Marisala realized that Liam had taken one look at her dressed up like a stranger, on her very best behavior, with her makeup carefully applied, hair carefully done, nails carefully polished, and he'd decided that not only did he want her in his bed, but he wanted her there forever.

She didn't know whether to laugh or cry.

She tried to tell herself that it didn't matter. She was getting what she wanted—a chance to be Liam's lover. If she had known dressing up like this would give her this kind of response, she would have done it years ago.

The movement of his eyes sweeping down her body was as tangible as a caress. She could see his desire for her etched onto his face, giving him a wolflike, hungry look. He unfastened his bow tie and then his cummerbund, and then the tiny, shiny buttons of his tuxedo shirt, moving slowly now, all the while watching her.

She reached up to unhook her bra, watching him watch her, aware that she was breathing much too quickly, aware of him gazing at the tops of her breasts as they rose and fell, at last free from the ultra-sexy bra she'd bought for him. Would he look at her that way if she were wearing her cotton underwear? She didn't like feeling this doubt.

Liam looked up into her eyes and smiled, a fierce, scaldingly hot smile as he pulled his shirttail from his pants and his arms from his sleeves. "Maybe we should go upstairs."

His smile wasn't enough to reassure her. Dreadfully uncertain, Marisala remembered the words Liam himself had told her over and over again. When in a social situation, and you don't know what to say or do, let the other person lead. Well, this wasn't quite the social situation he'd been talking about, but letting him lead seemed the best thing to do.

"If you want."

"What do *you* want?"

"I want whatever you want. I want to please you." She didn't dare be more specific, although she would have liked to be. She couldn't remember ever being so ill at ease with him. He wanted to make love to the woman in the black party dress. Mother of God, he wanted to *marry* that woman. But she didn't know who that woman was. All she knew was that it wasn't really her.

He stood up and she let him lead her up the stairs, up to his bedroom.

Her words had been a lie. She didn't want to go upstairs. She didn't want to take the time. She'd wanted him right there, in the living room. She wanted him on the stairs, standing up. She wanted him in the hall, right on the floor.

But she was letting him lead, and he led her to his bed.

"Do you want me to put on some music?" he asked.

She could see his arousal straining hard against the fabric of his pants. How could he think about music right now? How could he want anything but to rid them both of the rest of their clothes and to bury himself deeply inside of her?

She wanted to push him down onto his back and straddle him, impaling herself on him, leading them to ecstasy. She wanted to spread herself wide and guide him to her, but she didn't. She slowly sat down on his bed, afraid to take control of their lovemaking, afraid to do anything for fear she would give herself away.

"Are you all right?" he asked, sitting down on the other side of the bed. "You're so quiet, are you sure you want to do this?"

She had to laugh at the irony. "Do I want to? God, I'm sitting here, *dying* for you to touch me!"

He reached for her and she fell into his arms, pushing them both down onto his bed as he kissed her. The sensation of his skin against hers made her moan as she slid her hands along the hard muscles of his shoulders and back.

He was touching her everywhere, and kissing her everywhere else. The feeling of his body on top of her, the weight of his legs intertwined with hers set her on fire.

She felt him slip his hands between them and unfasten the button of his pants. She moved to help him, working his zipper down and filling her hands with all of him.

But he pulled back, out of her reach, as he worked to rid her of the remaining scrap of satin and lace she'd taken such pains to wear for him.

She sat up, wanting to touch him again, wanting to push his pants down his legs, wanting to see all of him.

He was so beautiful—so hard and muscular and utterly, thoroughly male.

But he stopped her, pulling away again. "I want to look at you," he murmured.

She throbbed with need, but she obediently did as he asked and lay back against his sheets and pillows, letting her legs fall open, willing him to touch her, but again, afraid to ask. She was afraid to be demanding, afraid he wouldn't want her if she was.

But then he did touch her. He trailed his fingers and his mouth lightly down her body, driving her half-mad with desire.

"Please," she gasped as he touched her in her most intimate place, finding her slick and ready for him. "Liam, please!"

This time when she reached for him, he didn't move away. This time he let her caress him, and she realized he'd already covered himself with a condom, taking precautions to protect them both. But then, with a groan, he pulled her hands away from him, pinning them up above her head, pressing himself down on top of her. Marisala shifted her hips, searching for him, wanting him, needing him *now*. . . .

"Mara, look at me," he commanded, and she opened her eyes.

His face was so familiar, so dear, and when he gave her one of his crooked smiles, she thought her heart might burst. It was an overwhelming sensation, and it overpowered everything she felt, even the tempest of her desire.

"It's been a while for me," he admitted raggedly.

"And . . ." He took a deep breath. "And I want you so much I know I'm going to embarrass myself. And all I keep thinking is, God, I better not. I better do this right, or you're not going to want to marry me."

He tried to laugh, tried to pretend that it was funny, but she could see in his eyes just how important this was to him.

"You don't actually think I'd base a decision like that on one time and only one time, do you?" she teased. "Even in baseball, you get three strikes before you're out."

His laughter was more genuine now. "That's a relief." But still he hesitated, just gazing down at her. "I want you to be my wife," he finally said. "I need you, Mara. When I saw you tonight, I . . . It was just so obvious. I'm sorry it took me so long to realize the truth."

The truth. He'd found what he thought was the truth from her deceit, from her dress-up games. He didn't truly want her—he wanted the woman he thought her to be.

But there was one truth she'd discovered tonight while looking into Liam's eyes. "I love you," she whispered. It was true. She loved him—completely, absolutely, and endlessly. She always had and she always would.

"I know. I wasn't sure *you* knew, but . . . I did. I knew you were mine a long time ago," he told her quietly. "Now all you have to do is tell me, yes, you'll marry me."

She wanted to hear more from him. She wanted to

hear him say he loved her too. He wanted her. He *needed* her. It wasn't enough.

"Yes, I'll marry you," she said very softly. She didn't want to give in—but she knew she had no choice. As miserable as she would be to lose her identity through marriage, she knew she'd be twice as miserable without Liam.

He kissed her slowly and so sweetly. And then, still taking his time, he pressed himself so perfectly inside of her, finally joining their bodies as completely as their hearts.

She could hear him breathing hard, trying to control himself. But she didn't want him in control. She wanted him wild and frantic. She wanted him as lost in his passion for her as she was for him.

She lifted her hips, driving him more deeply inside of her, pulling his mouth down to hers for another kiss, a harder, hungry kiss. She felt more than heard him groan as he began to move, first matching her rhythm, then kicking it even higher.

"Mara—" He tried to slow them down, but she pushed him even faster. Yes, this was what she wanted.

She felt his shuddering release, heard her name in his ragged, breathless cry. She gripped him tightly as his name, too, was ripped from her throat, as she, too, exploded with wave upon scorching wave of pleasure that shook her until she trembled, until she lay exhausted, her face buried in the warmth of Liam's neck.

And then there was only silence. Minutes passed, and Marisala started to float, half-asleep. Liam was no lightweight, but she loved the sensation of his body still on top of hers. She hoped he would stay there, still inside of her, all night long.

But finally he stirred and rolled off her, pulling her into his arms. "That was incredible," he murmured. "Do you always do that? It was unreal. . . ." He paused. "It *was* real, wasn't it? I mean, you weren't just trying to keep me from being embarrassed because I, you know, couldn't stop myself from . . ."

Marisala opened her eyes and looked up at him. "Real?" she repeated, not quite understanding. "You don't think I'd actually just *pretend* to? . . . "

"Some women do. They fake it so the man doesn't feel bad. And the guy never even knows that it's not the real thing." He smiled sleepily down at her. "You've honestly never done that?"

Marisala shook her head no.

He kissed her. "Good. Don't start, okay? I like the real thing."

He pulled her so that her back was pressed against his front, and draping one arm possessively across her, he sighed. "Let's get married over Thanksgiving break." His voice was distant as if sleep were very near. "We can go down to San Salustiano, have the ceremony there."

"If that's what you want," Marisala whispered.

"Yeah. I want to make love to you in the moonlight, on the beach. And up in the mountains too. I want to take you back there as my wife."

Emotion closed her throat and she couldn't speak.

"My wife." He sighed again, his breathing slow and steady as he drifted into sleep.

He wanted her to be his wife. Or did he? He had been drawn to the way she'd looked tonight, the way she'd walked and talked and acted. But that wasn't her. That wasn't the real thing.

It wasn't even close.

TEN

Liam knew as soon as he opened the door that there was going to be trouble.

The man standing there was in his early thirties, and he was accompanied by two little girls—a four-year-old and another, slightly older, maybe a second grader.

The man held out his hand. "Ron Hughes," he introduced himself. "We're here about Fluffy."

"Fluffy?"

"Hi, I'm Marisala. We spoke on the phone." Liam turned to see Mara coming down the stairs, Evita in her arms.

The smaller of the two girls let out a shriek. "Fluffy! Daddy, it's Fluffy!"

Evita let out an excited bark, and Marisala set the puppy on the floor.

Little girl and puppy met in a tangled heap of arms, legs, and paws. The older girl soon joined the pile.

"Sally's right, Daddy," she called out joyfully. "It *is* Fluffy!"

"It looks like you found our dog," Ron said cheerfully.

Liam's heart sank and he swore silently. He *knew* this was going to happen. He'd *told* Marisala. . . .

She was sitting on the stairs, arms wrapped tightly around her knees as she watched the two girls hugging the puppy she had come to love.

"I've never done this before," Liam told Ron, "and I'm not sure how we go about proving the dog's yours. Do you have papers or pictures or—"

"The dog is theirs, Liam," Marisala said quietly. "Look at them. The dog is theirs."

Ron reached for his wallet. "I'm prepared to pay a reward, of course."

Liam's temper flared. "We don't want your money. Although it might be nice to know how you could lose a puppy and not manage to find her until weeks later."

Ron lowered his voice, his eyes apologetic. "The girls' mother was in an accident while on a business trip in D.C. We had to fly down there to be with her while she was in the hospital. I got a neighbor to take Fluffy, but the dog managed to get free. I do appreciate your caring for her all this time, and I'd like to reimburse you for—"

"Is your wife all right?" Marisala had come to stand beside him. Liam slipped his arm around her shoulder, and she pressed herself against him, as if she needed his solidness and his warmth.

"She's got a pin in her hip, but she's going to be

okay." Ron had his wallet out again. "Please, I'd like to repay you—"

"Send a donation to the Boston Refugee Center," Marisala told him. "That would be a good way to repay us."

Ron nodded. "I'll do that." He looked down at Fluffy and his daughters still giggling together on the floor. "Well, I guess we better get going."

Marisala started toward the kitchen. "I have a leash—"

"That's okay, I brought one." Ron drew a leather-and-chain leash from his jacket pocket. "Come on, girls."

The two blond cherubs stood up, and the puppy, ever playful, ran in circles around them. She took a spin around Liam, too, then skittered into the kitchen.

"Fluffy, come back!" the smaller girl started after her.

"I'll get her," Marisala told the child. She went into the kitchen, calling the puppy to her in Spanish.

The older girl's eyes were wide. "Does Fluffy speak French?" she asked her father.

"That's Spanish, Ashley. And yeah, after a couple of weeks she probably understands quite a bit."

Marisala came out of the kitchen, Evita—Fluffy—in her arms. As Liam watched she kissed the top of the puppy's head before setting her on the floor and helping Ron attach the leash to her collar.

She looked up at the two girls. "You take care of . . . Fluffy for me, okay?"

They nodded.

"Treat her nicely and give her lots of hugs. I know you will, right?"

Another nod.

"Good." Marisala straightened up.

"Thanks again," Ron told them both as he led the puppy and his daughters out into the hall.

The door closed behind them, and they were gone.

Marisala looked at Liam and forced a smile. "What a nice family."

"Are you all right?"

"I'm fine. You told me this would happen, and . . . I'm fine."

Santiago wouldn't have recognized her. She was wearing one of her pretty cotton dresses again today. Liam hadn't seen her in her trademark shorts and tank top in days. Not since the night of the ball—the night they'd first made love.

She'd spent every night since then in his bed, and some long, delicious mornings too. It was funny, but Marisala was more shy than he would have imagined, more restrained than he would have thought when it came to making love. But her only other lover had been a man from San Salustiano. It was possible Enrique had been controlling. Perhaps she'd learned to be so passive from him.

But it didn't matter. She was going to marry Liam. They had all the time in the world to truly learn to please each other in bed. They had a lifetime.

He reached for her. "We could get another puppy."

"No. Thank you, but no." She stood for a moment in his embrace, but then pulled away.

This was weird. He'd expected tears and an outpouring of emotion and pain, not this cool, much too mature acceptance of the situation. It was as if someone had kidnapped Marisala and replaced her with one of the Stepford Wives.

She smiled at him again and he realized she was wearing makeup and her hair was neatly combed and pulled back from her face. "I'll be upstairs. I have some letters to write."

Liam watched her go up the stairs, watched her hips swaying gently beneath the fabric of her dress. He heard the door to her room close, heard her switch on the radio he'd bought for her. That, at least, was still tuned to the rhythmic sounds of the local Spanish station.

He stood there for a long time, unable to shake his feeling of unease.

Marisala held the jeweler's box, knowing well what was inside.

An engagement ring.

Liam was watching her, expectation and anticipation simmering in his eyes.

She didn't want an engagement ring. She didn't want a diamond. She didn't want to wear a ring on her finger, a symbol of love, yes, but a symbol of imprisonment too.

"Open it," Liam urged her. He was leaning back, propped up on one elbow, his hair a disheveled jumble of waves and curls, messed from their recent lovemaking.

She knelt on the bed, leaning forward slightly as she opened the box, so that her hair fell over her face. She didn't want him to see her first reaction to the ring. Although she was getting quite good at hiding her feelings, she didn't think she could handle this.

But he reached for her, sweeping her hair back from her face with one hand.

Marisala steeled herself and . . .

It wasn't a diamond.

It wasn't a traditional engagement ring at all.

It was silver and handcrafted. And in the center of the band was a roughly cut and only partially polished, very small ocean-colored stone.

"It's turquoise," Liam told her. "It was made by a guy I know from Montana—a Native American artisan, a Navajo."

"It's beautiful," Marisala breathed.

"I figured you wouldn't want to wear a ring all the time, but I *did* want to get you an engagement gift, and I thought—"

Marisala threw her arms around him and kissed him.

He laughed. "Does that mean you like it?"

"I love it." She took it from the box and put it on her finger. It fit perfectly. She could feel tears welling in her eyes, feel emotion crowding the back of her throat. "How did you know?"

His eyes were almost the exact same shade of blue as the stone in the ring. "Oh, come on, Mara, it wasn't that hard. You've got to figure I know you pretty well by now."

"Do you?"

Something shifted in his eyes. "Why, don't you think I do?"

"I don't know."

He shifted, sitting up to look at her. "My God, are you crying?"

"No." She turned away.

He caught her arm. "You are. Marisala, what's the matter?"

"I'm crying because I'm so happy," she lied. She reached for him. "Liam, make love to me again."

Sex was the only thing she was certain of. She knew that she turned him on, even though she was still careful to let him lead. She knew he couldn't resist the sweet invitation of her body.

She could feel his immediate response to her as he drew her into his arms and kissed her.

"Inez will wonder why we've spent all day upstairs."

Marisala had to laugh at that as she wiped her tears away. "Inez won't wonder at all. She sees the way I look at you."

"And the way I look at you." He kissed her again, pulling her on top of him as he lay on his back. "Don't you have a class or something this afternoon?"

"It doesn't matter," Marisala told him. "It's all foolishness anyway."

"Whereas making love is *very* serious business," he teased.

Marisala kissed him, shifting her hips so that they melted into one, and just like that his teasing stopped.

Marisala sat with Liam at Ricardo Montoya's Thursday-night meeting at the Refugee Center.

This was the second meeting they had come to, and like the first time, Liam sat near the back and did little more than listen.

Listening was good, but what Liam had to do was talk.

Halfway through the session, he excused himself quietly and disappeared.

After fifteen minutes passed, Marisala went looking for him.

She found him sitting on the steps out in front of the Refugee Center, watching the people walk by in the cool evening air.

"You've been out here for a while," she said.

Liam nodded, turning to smile up at her as if he hadn't a care in the world. God, he was good at doing that. "Yeah."

"Maybe you should try coming back inside."

He didn't move. "I know. I should."

Marisala sat down next to him, smoothing the skirt of her dress over her knees.

"I like it when you wear dresses," he said, slipping his arm around her shoulder.

"I know."

He nuzzled her neck. "You wear them for me, don't you?"

"Yes."

"I like knowing that too. It turns me on." He pulled her chin toward him, covering her mouth in a long, slow kiss.

Marisala knew what he was doing. He was trying his best to distract them both. It was working. She took a deep breath as she pulled away from him. "Come back inside."

He made circles with his thumb on the palm of her hand as he gave her his best bedroom smile. "I'd rather go home and make love to you."

It was impossible to resist him. She closed her eyes as he kissed her neck again. "I would too."

But he didn't stand up to go back inside, or to go home. "I'm not doing very well with these meetings, am I?"

Marisala opened her eyes to find him still smiling at her. His smile had a touch of chagrin, but everything else he was feeling was very neatly concealed.

"You're doing fine."

"I'm not doing fine. I'm sitting outside." He paused. "Why aren't you yelling at me for copping out?"

She hesitated. "Because . . . you're trying your best?"

He laughed and said something extremely obscene. "This isn't my best." And just like that, he wasn't laughing any longer. Just like that, the easygoing, laid-back front he always wore was stripped away, exposing the very uncertain, very frustrated, very angry and frightened man underneath. "This is just sitting on the stairs because I'm scared to death of—"

He stopped himself. "I'm sorry." As Marisala watched he took a deep breath and hid nearly all of his fear and frustration behind a smile.

It was all she could do to keep from grabbing him

and shaking him. Don't stop, she wanted to shout at him. Keep going, keep talking! But instead, she kept her voice calm. "Don't apologize for being honest."

He was silent, just staring out at the street.

"Come back inside," she finally said again.

Liam managed another smile, but shook his head. "I . . . can't."

She stood up. "All right. Then let's go home. Maybe next week—"

"No, Mara, I need . . ." Liam rubbed his forehead in frustration. He needed her to shout at him. Some things needed to be shouted about, she'd told him. Why couldn't she see that this was one of them? He didn't need her gentle understanding. He needed her outrage, her scorn. He'd told her he would attend these meetings. He'd told her he wanted to try to talk about everything he'd been through. He needed her to throw that in his face, to toss out a challenge, to fight for him— even if the enemy was his own self, his own weakness.

But she was backing away from him again, tiptoeing around him the way she had been for weeks now.

At the same time what was he doing, blaming her for his own shortcomings? He knew he and he alone had to take responsibility for his life. If he wanted changes, he had to stand up and face the darkness he'd hidden from for so long. Marisala couldn't do that for him.

And maybe that's why she was pulling away from him. Maybe after two weeks of watching him come to these group sessions and *still* be unable to talk, she was doubting his ability to change. Maybe she was realizing he'd never be the man he was before he'd been thrown into hell. Maybe she dreaded the thought of a lifetime filled with nightmares.

Although, the nightmares weren't as bad with Marisala in his bed. He still woke up far too often with his heart pounding and his mouth dry. But his need to light every corner of his condo when he awoke in the night had let up.

She was still watching him. He wanted to take her into his arms and beg her never to let him go. But he knew he'd sound pathetic and that could very well drive her further away.

She held out her hand. "Let's go home," she said again.

"No." Liam stood up, straightening his shoulders and back. "I'm going back inside." He knew he wasn't going to talk. He knew he was just going to listen, but that was better than nothing, right?

He hoped Marisala would think so too.

Marisala made tea while Inez sat at the kitchen table, her baby to her breast.

"I hope William's crying didn't wake you," Inez said.

"It didn't." Marisala pulled all the boxes of herbal tea down from the shelf, unable to decide which blend to have. "Liam fell asleep early, but I was still up."

He'd come home from Rico's group session exhausted, even though he hadn't said a single word all night long. Despite his smiling exterior, she knew this was so hard for him, she was starting to wonder if it was, in fact, worth it.

"Have you bought a dress for your wedding?" Inez asked.

A wedding dress. God. That was the last thing on her mind.

"I can picture you in one of those long gowns." Inez smiled dreamily. "With a long train trailing after you. You'll look so beautiful—Liam will think he's marrying a princess."

Marisala turned away, struck by Inez's innocent words. Liam already thought he was marrying some kind of princess. She'd fooled him into thinking she was something more than what she really was that night of the charity ball.

Ever since then, she'd been working to maintain the masquerade, but every day she could feel herself slipping.

Marisala poured hot water over her tea bag, fighting back her tears. She had been crazy to agree to marry Liam. Had she honestly expected to be able to spend the entire rest of her life pretending to be someone she was not?

And she was not this person that Liam wanted to marry. She was not refined and elegant and calm and cool. She was no longer able to stand back and wait for him to take the lead in their conversations, in their life, in their *lovemaking*.

Mother of God, she sometimes thought she'd go mad if she had to wait, passively, for him to touch her one more time. Sometimes she thought she'd go mad if she had to keep herself from talking to him—*really* talking to him. Do you love me? She wanted to ask him, but she didn't dare.

Because a quiet, humble, *civilized* woman was the kind of woman Liam wanted. Marisala was afraid if she acted otherwise, if she spoke out whenever she wanted, then he wouldn't want her anymore.

So he wanted her. Maybe he even loved her. But even if he did, it wasn't really her that he loved.

Marisala was as unhappy as she'd ever been. And the guilt of what she'd done, of how she had tricked him— was still tricking him—churned in her stomach, making her feel queasy and ill.

And Liam was unhappy too. She'd seen him watching her intently, frowning slightly when he thought she wasn't looking. Clearly, he saw through her facade, and he was wondering where that woman who had come to the ball in the black dress had gone.

She loved him more than she'd ever dreamed possible. She loved him enough to know that she couldn't keep lying to him.

She turned and smiled at Inez, trying to hide all of her pain and sorrow, just the way Liam always did. "I'll be upstairs if you need me."

Inez blinked. "But your tea . . ."

Marisala was already out the door. "Good night."

She went up the stairs, moving quickly past the temptation of Liam's bedroom. She went into the room where she still kept her clothes, and in a deceptively calm voice—Liam and Santiago both would have been very proud—she called for a taxi to come and pick her up.

And then she began to pack her clothes.

Her clothes only.

If she never saw those dresses Liam had bought for her again, it wouldn't be soon enough.

Liam, however, would be much, much harder to forget.

ELEVEN

The light was on downstairs.

Liam had awoken from a nightmare to find himself alone in his bed, and his first thought had been that Marisala was finally gone.

He'd known something big was coming for at least a week now. Marisala had been acting so oddly. And now he knew the reason why. She hadn't been happy. She'd wanted to leave.

But then he saw the light and he heard voices, and he realized he was mistaken. It was barely even midnight, and Marisala was in the kitchen, talking as Inez fed the baby.

Liam pulled on his robe and went down the stairs, trying to calm his pounding heart. Everything was fine. Marisala was fine. It was simply his overactive imagination going paranoid on him. It was merely an extension of his bad dreams and . . .

Marisala stood in the entryway. She was dressed for

going out into the cool autumn night, her suitcase at her side.

Liam froze halfway down the stairs, his worst fears realized as he stared at that suitcase. She was leaving.

From the corner of his eye he saw Inez fade back into the kitchen. He looked up from that suitcase and saw the truth echoed in Marisala's eyes. She *was* leaving.

Somehow, Liam managed to remain standing. Somehow he remained alive, and astonishingly able to function. He forced his voice to sound light. "What, no farewell note?"

Her voice shook. "I was going to call you in the morning. To explain."

"I guess this means you don't want to marry me."

She shook her head, fighting her tears. "No."

Liam nodded. He didn't blame her. He'd failed her, and himself as well, and now she was going to leave. This was his fault. He'd seen it coming, and yet he'd done nothing to prevent it. He hadn't even had the courage to confront her, to talk about it. "I'm sorry," he said, but his voice sounded empty and emotionless—as if he were commenting on the weather.

"I can't do this anymore," she told him, emotion making her voice tremble. "I can't wear the clothes you want me to wear. I can't pretend to be someone I'm not for the entire rest of my life!"

Her words didn't make sense. "Clothes?"

"I feel like such a liar!" With a sob, Marisala yanked open the door. Grabbing her suitcase, she headed for the elevators.

Liam followed, bare feet, bathrobe, and all. "Mara, what are you talking about?"

She savagely punched the elevator's call button. The doors slid open almost immediately.

"I was a fool," she told him as she stepped into the elevator. "I knew from the start that I wouldn't be a good wife for you, still I tried to pretend it would work. But I can't bear to wear those clothes anymore, or to act as if I don't have any kind of opinion. I know you liked me that way, and I tried, I *really* tried to be the woman you wanted. But I can't do it anymore."

Liam followed her. "Mara—"

She pressed the button that held the doors open. "Get out, Liam. You don't ride in elevators, remember?"

"I'll learn to handle it," he told her. He pulled her hand away from the controls and the doors slid shut. "See, I'm learning already."

She wrenched herself from his grasp and opened the door again. "I don't want you to learn to *handle* anything! I don't want you to hide what you feel! I want you to stop fighting your memories. God, we are *both* such liars." She grabbed her suitcase and got off the elevator, heading instead for the stairs.

Liam chased her down the stairs. "Mara, don't leave—I don't understand. Talk to me!"

She whirled to face him. "I don't want to talk to you. I don't want *you* to talk to *me*. I want you to stand up on a table and scream. If I were you, I'd kick over chairs and stop people on the street to shout about the horrible things human beings can do to one another in the name of politics. But you have taught yourself so carefully to let nothing escape! No feelings, no emotions. You hold yourself in such careful control—is it any wonder you can't write?

"What a pair we are. You go to your meetings and you sit there, pretending to listen. But I know what you're doing. You're still fighting the memories. On the surface, you're so calm and in control, but I know you, remember? I know that you have all those nightmares inside of you, fighting to break free."

What could he say? Her accusations were all right on the money.

She started down the stairs again. "Of course, I'm no better than you. I'm as big a liar as you are. You're the one man I'd trade my future for." Her words came out in sobs, and she could no longer hold back her tears. "You're the one man I'd sacrifice *everything* for, just to be with. I might even be able to live with the lies I've told myself, but I can't handle the lies I've told to you. Mother of God, between the two of us, Liam, I feel as if I'm drowning in an ocean of deceit!"

She pushed open the door that led out onto the sidewalk, and Liam saw there was a cab waiting there for her.

"I'm not that woman in the black dress you met at the charity ball," she told him tearfully. "And I'll never be."

Suddenly everything she was saying clicked. And just like that, it all made sense. The clothes, the hair, the careful way she'd been acting over the past few weeks.

Marisala had actually thought Liam had wanted her to be someone other than herself.

"Mara, God, you are *so* wrong about—"

She opened the door to the cab. "And you know what hurts the most? It's stupid, really, but you never bothered to tell me that you love me. You kept that hidden inside too."

She climbed into the cab, locking the door behind her, shutting him out.

"Wait," he said. "Wait!"

But she motioned for the driver to leave.

"I love you," he told her, banging on the window as the cab pulled away. But she didn't turn around, didn't even glance in his direction.

Liam's car was on the street—he'd gotten another great parking spot last night. He ran toward it, thinking he could follow, but his keys were up on the top of his dresser. Without them, he was going nowhere.

All he could do was stand in the street in his bathrobe and watch the cab's taillights disappear.

The real irony was that she had been trying so hard to be like him.

He should have been taking lessons from her instead.

"I love you!" he shouted, but it was far too late.

Marisala was gone.

"Sorry, man, I can't help you. She's not here."

Liam looked directly into Dan's eyes. "Would you tell me if she was?"

"No. Probably not. But she's *not* here."

"I just want to know that she's safe. Can you tell me if you know that she's safe?"

"I haven't seen her," Dan said, opening the screen door and stepping out onto the porch. "I wish she *had* come to me, but she didn't. Saturday mornings, she usually goes to the library—did you look there?"

"She didn't show. She didn't go to any of her classes yesterday, either." Liam sat down on the steps, the fatigue from almost forty-eight hours without any sleep catching up to him in an overpowering wave. "I don't know where to look. She could be *anywhere*."

Dan sat down next to him, lit a cigarette, and took a deep drag. He turned his head away as he blew out a long stream of smoke. "Did you try that guy from the Refugee Center? Ricardo something? She introduced me to him a few weeks ago at an Amnesty International meeting. They seemed pretty tight."

"I don't know where he lives. His home phone's unlisted—I have the number but I have no way of getting his address. And his answering machine says he's away for the weekend. I left about twelve messages, I even called the Refugee Center, but . . ." He ran his hands down his face in frustration.

"So why did she leave? Whad'ya do?" Dan asked bluntly, squinting through his cigarette smoke. "Get medieval on her, try to order her around, tell her what to do?"

"No," Liam said. "I asked her to marry me."

Dan tried to hide a laugh and failed. "Sorry," he apologized. "I don't get it," he added. "She's crazy about you. I should know—I tried to get her out of your evil clutches more times than you probably want to hear about, but she let me know, no doubt about it, that she was doing fine right where she was."

"I think she only agreed to marry me to make me happy," Liam said. "In San Salustiano, marriage isn't an equal partnership. Women don't have many choices to start with, and after they marry, their husbands make all the decisions. I think she thought we would have that kind of relationship, because when I went through her desk and the notebooks that she left behind, I found a copy of a letter she sent to the university about her admission to medical school. She told them she wouldn't be applying because she was getting married. I think she thought I would want her to leave school."

"Would you?"

"No!"

Dan took one last drag on his cigarette then crushed the butt beneath his boot. "Obviously you and she have had some kind of communication breakdown."

Liam shot the other man a look. "No kidding, Dr. Freud."

"And as long as I'm pointing fingers, might I mention the total un-coolness of you going through her desk and notebooks?"

"I was looking for some kind of clue as to where she went. I wasn't just randomly snooping."

A trolley car went past, rattling noisily on the tracks that ran in the middle of Commonwealth Avenue. Dan watched as it stopped, let several passengers off, then continued on its way. "I don't know Marisala that well, but something tells me if she doesn't want you to find her, she's not going to be easy to find."

"So what are you suggesting? That I just sit around and wait for her to come back?"

"I'm suggesting that you've got your job cut out for you." Dan appraised him coolly. "But you're some kind of crack investigative reporter, right? This should be right up your alley."

"I *was* an investigative reporter," Liam told him. "But for the past few years I've written nothing but Sunday columns." He snorted, disgusted with himself. "And for the past few months I've written nothing new at all."

Liam froze. Wait a minute. What had he just said? Nothing but . . .

Sunday columns.

"My God." He turned to Dan. "I need to use your phone."

Dan stood up. "Why? You figure out where Marisala is?"

"No." Liam stood up too. "But I've figured out how to find her."

"Let's see if I've got this straight." On the other end of the telephone wire, Lauren Stuart was coming the closest Liam had ever heard to losing her cool. "You want me to stop the presses for a column you *haven't even written yet?*"

"Two hours," Liam said. "Come on, Stuart. How often have I asked you for a favor like this?"

"Never—obviously this is the first time you've ever gone *clear out of your mind*!"

"Please, Lauren, this is life-and-death. I'm not sure I'll be able to live until next Sunday. Damn, I'm not sure I'm going to make it to tomorrow."

Silence. Liam closed his eyes and prayed.

His editor sighed and swore. "You know I can't give you two hours, but if you can get me the column on disk in one hour—"

"An *hour*! God, I'm fifteen minutes away from the office as it is!"

"That's the best I can do for you, Lee. Take it or leave it."

Liam looked up at Dan. "You got a pen and some kind of paper—a legal pad or something that I can borrow?"

"Yeah." Dan disappeared into the other room.

Liam took a deep breath. "I'll have it for you in an hour."

"I can't wait even a minute longer," Lauren told him. "If you're not here, if it's not in my hand, you're out of luck."

"I'm on my way." Liam nodded his thanks to Dan, who'd returned with a yellow pad and a cheap blue pen.

"Lee, wait—keep the word count down to around seven hundred. Oh, and can you at least give me a hint as to the topic?"

Liam told her.

Lauren cut off her own surprised silence. "Forget what I said about word count. Make it as long as you want. But I need it on my desk in an hour!"

———◆———

Marisala looked up as Ricardo's wife, Linda, cautiously knocked on the open door.

She didn't try to smile. There was no need to hide the fact that she was miserable. She'd sat up talking with both Linda and Ricardo until late the previous night. She'd told them everything.

Almost everything.

She *hadn't* told them how, without Liam by her side, she felt as if her heart had been torn from her chest. She hadn't told them how desolately her life stretched out in front of her. She hadn't told them that she would have liked—at least once—to have made love to Liam with all of the passion she carried inside of her.

"I brought you some coffee and a bagel. I hope you like cream cheese." Linda carried a tray heavily weighed down by a plastic-wrapped bundle. "And Rico thought you might want to see the Sunday paper?"

The *Globe*. Liam's paper.

"No," Marisala said. "I don't want to see it."

Linda set the tray down on the guest room's bedside table and hefted the heavy newspaper. "As you wish."

"Wait." Marisala closed her eyes. "Yes. I *do* want to see it. Please."

Linda handed her the plastic-wrapped paper with a smile.

"Maybe there's something in here about San Salustiano," Marisala continued, opening the bundle and searching for the editorial pages. "But of course you know that's not really why I want to look at the paper.

We *both* know I can't bear not to search for Liam's column and the little stupid picture they have of him in the corner, even though both the picture *and* the column are three years old and—"

SOME THINGS ARE WORTH SHOUTING ABOUT. The headline next to Liam's little picture was not one she had ever seen before.

At first she didn't believe it. It was only a headline. So they rewrote the headline of an article that had run before. Big deal.

Five years ago, I spent eighteen months of my life locked in the dark.

Marisala looked up at Linda in shock. "It's new. Liam wrote a new column."

For eighteen months I lived the uncertain life of a political prisoner in the deepest dungeon of a San Salustiano mountain prison. For eighteen months I was kept alive by my undying belief that justice would prevail, that democracy would be restored as the people of that tiny island nation rose up to reclaim a government that was for the people and by the people—not against the people. And for eighteen months I was sustained by my visions of an angel, a young girl who had tried to protect me and keep me from that very prison cell.

Marisala, you're not a girl anymore. You're a woman now, and you don't know it, but I fell in love with you the first night I met you. I didn't know it myself at the time, but what I felt for you was as strong and as pure as the truest of loves. I love you

still, not because of the way you look—and you are *the
most beautiful woman I've ever known, whether
you're dressed in a gunnysack or a designer gown
(secondhand, of course, Marisala. And no doubt bargained down to an acceptable price!). But I love you
because of your generous heart and stubborn pride and
your inability to stay quiet when injustice rears its
ugly head.*

She heard the door click as Linda left the room. But
it wasn't until she looked up that she realized her
friend's wife had left to give her privacy. Because
Marisala was crying. There were tears running like a
river down her face.

He loved her. Liam loved her. And he was *writing*
again. He was writing to her. An entire column in the
newspaper—just for *her.*

*You know I was tortured in prison even though I've
never talked about it. Men from the government and
the army came every so often to ask me questions
about the rebel guerrillas—about you and your
soldiers. They thought I knew more than I did, and
they would beat me and torment me to persuade me to
talk.*

*Of course, I had nothing to say—not to them,
anyway. And when they tossed me back into my dark,
stinking little cell, I would fight to stay alive, no matter how badly they had hurt me. Because I had hope—
hope that someday I would see your smile again. I was*

uncrushable. I was unbreakable because I had that powerful hope to keep my heart beating.

But then one day, they broke me.

I was brought up to the glaring brightness of the courtyard. But instead of questions and a beating, I was told that someone—a young girl—had been caught trying to smuggle some food and a message in to me.

I was terrified, because I was certain that girl was you. I demanded to see you, and the captain of the guards laughed in my face. He took great delight in telling me that the girl had been killed in the struggle with the guards. And then I saw your body, lying in the dust. I ran to you, but they stopped me before I reached you.

I didn't see your face, they never let me see your face, but I was certain that girl was you and that you were dead.

And that day, after they beat me and threw me back into the darkness, I lay on the floor and I tried to die. They'd crushed me, Mara. With you dead, my hope was gone.

But as empty as it was, my heart wouldn't stop beating, and four days later you were part of the rebel forces that broke down those prison walls and set us all free.

You were still alive. It wasn't you who had died that day. It was some other girl—someone else's hopes and dreams.

I lived in the darkness for eighteen months, but it

*was those last four days that damaged me nearly be-
yond repair. Because no man can live without hope.*

*Today my hope is that you'll come home. I'm
shouting from the tabletop, Mara. Please come home.*

Marisala put the paper down. She pulled back the
bedcovers, climbed into her clothes, and taking her suitcase, she headed for home.

TWELVE

Liam was sitting on the stairs when he heard the key turn in the lock. He knew it wasn't Hector or Inez. He'd lent them his car so they could spend the day out in Hartford, visiting with Inez's cousin, showing off baby William.

It had to be Marisala. Dear God, please let it be Marisala.

He stood up as the door opened, and . . .

She looked up at him as soon as she stepped inside. She was wearing jeans with holes in the knees and a leather jacket over an oversized T-shirt. Her hair was unbrushed and her face was pale and streaked from tears, and Liam was certain he had never seen her look more incredibly beautiful in his entire life.

He didn't bother to say hi. He simply jumped right in, Marisala-style. "I love you."

She smiled, her eyes welling up with tears that she

didn't try to hide from him as she set her suitcase on the tile floor. "I know. I read it in the *Globe*."

He moved down one step and then another. "I'm going to try, Mara. I'm going to try to talk about the prison. I'm going to try to write about it. I know that's not much of a promise—"

"It's enough for me."

"I'm terrified," he admitted. "I'm scared to death that once I open my mouth I won't be able to shut up. I'm scared that everything I've kept inside for all these years will avalanche and bury me alive."

"Then I'll dig you out."

He laughed, stepping down onto the foyer's tile floor. "I know you will. God knows you've dug me out before."

"I'll hold your hand when you want me to," she told him. "I'll sit with you when you write, if you want me to. I'll hold you all night long and keep the nightmares far away. If you want me to."

"I want."

She stepped toward him and all he had to do was open his arms and he was holding her, kissing her. He tasted the salt of her tears on her lips along with the sweetness of her love for him.

The sharp pull of desire was so familiar and so instant, and he kissed her again, fiercely claiming her. He knew she felt his arousal because she laughed.

"Now, this is what I like." She reached between them and cupped him boldly in her hand. "Real, solid proof of how badly you missed me."

Liam was shocked—Marisala had always been so reserved, so passive when it came to making love.

Her eyes were sparkling as she looked up at him, but the sparkle faded quickly along with her smile when she saw the look of surprise on his face.

"I'm sorry," she apologized quickly, stepping away from him, a blush tingeing her cheeks as she looked away. "I wasn't thinking. I didn't mean to—"

"Marisala." He caught her chin in his hand, lifting it so that she had to look him in the eye. "How could you think I wouldn't absolutely *love* for you to touch me that way? How could you think I wouldn't want you to show me how much you want me?"

Tears had filled her eyes again. "I thought—"

"I *know* what you thought. You thought you had to be different, that you had to change. You thought I didn't want you the way you are. You thought I wanted what Santiago wanted—someone to fade into the background, to do what you were told, to look pretty and stay silent when the men talk."

Liam brushed his lips across her mouth. "I am so sorry I didn't figure out what you were thinking," he continued. "I knew something was wrong. I knew you were unhappy, and you were acting so strangely, but . . ."

He kissed her again, harder this time. "You're all I've ever wanted." He turned her to face the mirror that was by the door. "You. Are exactly. Who. I want. *This* you. The you with the holes in your jeans. The you who's going to go to medical school and become the best doctor San Salustiano's ever had. The you with the messy hair." He shook her shoulders very slightly, and she laughed. "Baby, you may not be Santiago's idea of a perfect wife, but you're not marrying him, you're marrying *me*. You *are* going to marry me?"

Marisala looked into the mirror. She looked as if she'd been dragged down a mountain by a donkey, and he looked as if he hadn't slept since she'd left. Knowing Liam, he probably hadn't. His eyes were filled with fatigue and rimmed with red, but his smile was pure tentative hope.

"You can keep your own name if you want," he told her. "Hell, I'll take *your* name if that'll make you feel better. We're both young, we can wait to have kids until you're out of med school, if you want. Or if you think you don't want any children, I'm open to discussion. I'd like to have kids, but not if it's going to make you miserable, and I guess what I'm trying to say is that my concept of marriage involves discussion and sharing and—" He cut himself off. "You're very quiet. It makes me nervous when you're so quiet."

He turned her to face him and gazed imploringly down into her eyes. "Marry me. Take a chance and say you'll marry me. And then come upstairs and make love with me so that I can pass out afterward and sleep for about a week."

Marisala had to laugh. "Well, God, when you put it so romantically . . ."

He kissed her, his unshaven face rasping sensuously against her cheeks. "Say yes."

Liam kissed her again, trying to melt away the reserve he could still see lingering in her eyes. "You know,

I was prepared to make any kind of compromise necessary," he told her. "I was ready to tell you, okay, we don't have to get married. We can simply live together for the rest of our lives. I was ready to say that all I want is to be with you, but that's not true. I want us to share what we've got. I want to jump onto that figurative tabletop and shout to God and the world that you own me, and I own you."

She smiled and kissed him, but still she didn't answer. She didn't say yes.

"Tell me what you're thinking," Liam implored. "Tell me what's holding you back."

"Sex."

He nearly choked. "What?"

"You know what I want?"

"Please tell me."

"I want to make love to you," Marisala told him. "And then, after we make love—after *I* make love to *you*—then if you still want to marry me, you can ask me again."

Liam had to laugh. "Well, hey, let me think this over. . . . Yes. I can go for this. Definitely."

"Are Hector and Inez home?"

"No, they're—"

"Good. Go upstairs and take a shower. And shave. And meet me in the living room in ten minutes." She kissed him. "Bring a condom."

The living room? "But . . ."

She was already all the way up the stairs, but she turned to look down at him. "I want to make love to you in every single room of this condo." She tried to hide her smile, but couldn't. "I thought we'd start with the living room."

"But . . ." Liam started up the stairs after her, but she'd already gone into her room and closed the door.

He tried the knob, but she'd locked it.

Buzzing with anticipation, he took the quickest shower of his life, spending most of those ten minutes she'd allotted him shaving the rough stubble from his cheeks and chin.

His bathrobe was nowhere to be found, so he pulled on a pair of sweatshorts. He slipped a condom into his pocket and headed downstairs.

Marisala was waiting for him, wearing his missing bathrobe. Her hair was damp from her own shower, and it hung in dark curls around her shoulders and down her back. She was sitting by the window, and as he came into the room she pulled the blinds, dimming the room and giving them privacy from the outside.

"Come here," she said.

He did.

She stood up, and he reached for her, pushing the robe from her shoulders even as she untied the belt.

She was so beautiful. The sight of her naked body still left him breathless.

She reached for him then, too, her hands slipping underneath the elastic waistband of his shorts and gliding down over his rear end as she pulled him closer. She kissed him, boldly claiming his mouth and pressing herself against him.

Liam heard himself groan as he filled his own hands

with the satiny smoothness of her skin. She opened herself to him, guiding one of his hands down to touch her.

"You know what I want?" she whispered.

"God, I hope I do."

She laughed. "I want you to sit on the couch."

"I want to take you right now, just like this, standing up," he countered.

"Hmm. That's a good idea too." Her hands swept around to the front of his shorts and her fingers closed around him.

God, he'd loved making love to her even when she was holding back—and she *had* been holding back, that much was clear. But this was off the scale. This was . . .

In one swift movement, she'd freed him from the confines of his shorts, pushing them down his legs. But now she knelt in front of him, and giving him a decidedly wicked smile, she touched him with the softness of her mouth, and sent him through the roof.

"Do you like that?" she finally asked, just as he knew he couldn't take any more. Her midnight eyes were laughing up at him. She knew quite well the answer to her question.

He could barely speak. "Oh, yeah."

"Good, because I do too."

Somehow she'd found the condom packet he'd been carrying in his shorts. She ripped it open, and pushing him back onto the couch, she covered him with it.

Liam couldn't wait another second. He grabbed her arms and hauled her up on top of him. She sensed his need and didn't hesitate, letting him guide her swiftly, fiercely down onto him.

She cried out as he filled her, clinging to him, her obvious pleasure pushing him dangerously close to the edge. He lay back on the couch so that he could fill her even more as she moved on top of him, setting a fast, hard pace.

He'd never dreamed that making love could be this good. This was the real Marisala, this wildcat in his arms. This was the woman he'd fallen in love with, the woman who spoke her mind and lived every moment of her life with pure, unrestrained passion.

It was such an odd feeling—this tenderness in his chest combined with the heart-attack sensation of the most incredible sex he'd ever experienced.

Not sex. Love. This was love unlike any he'd felt before. His heart was so full, it felt about to burst.

She took his hands, pressing them against the sweet swell of her breasts as she smiled down at him.

It was her smile that did it, her beautiful, wonderful smile that sent him roaring into orbit. And, as if she had been waiting for him, he felt her sudden release. She shouted her pleasure and it echoed around them as together they escaped the confines of gravity and shattered into a million perfect pieces.

Liam floated back to earth. None of his muscles seemed to be working. They had all turned to Jell-O.

A strand of Marisala's hair tickled his nose, but he couldn't move his hand to push it away. Besides, he liked the sensation. He liked that she was lying on top of him, seemingly as depleted and satisfied as he was.

"So," he said. His vocal cords still worked. That was good. "Let me see if I can figure out exactly *what* you were thinking. You thought maybe I'd have the best sex of my entire life and then *not* want to marry you?"

Marisala lifted her head, pulling her hair back from both of their faces. "I wasn't sure if you'd like me being so . . . aggressive."

He ran his finger down the side of her face. "Well, I'm not sure I'm about to go out and buy you a collection of whips and chains, but I'm up for just about anything else."

She laughed. "That's good."

"Oh, yeah." He let her see the heat he knew was lingering in his eyes. God, he was already starting to get hard again, just *thinking* about it. "So . . . will you marry me? Wait," he said, putting a finger across her lips. "Don't answer that. I seriously think we have to try this again. You know, make sure it wasn't just a freak occurrence?"

Marisala laughed, leaning forward to kiss him. "Are you kidding? You can't even move."

"Is that a challenge? Because you know I can't resist a challenge." With a groan, Liam sat up. He scooped her up off him, and holding her in his arms, he stood up. "My turn to pick the room, and I pick *my* room. *My* bed."

He carried her up the stairs. His tired muscles were aching, but he didn't give a damn.

Marisala was laughing as he threw her onto his bed.

"Yes," she said. "Yes. My answer is yes."

Liam fell back onto the bed with her and kissed her.

The afternoon sun sparkled in through the windows and reflected off the white ceiling, lighting his bedroom with a heavenly glow. He saw the same beautiful light in Marisala's eyes, and he knew that at last he'd come out of the darkness.

At long last, he'd come home.

EPILOGUE

The phone rang, and Liam picked it up.

Without hesitation, he reached for it. He lifted the receiver from the cradle.

" 'lo?" He tucked the receiver under his chin as he washed his hands in the kitchen sink, as if this was no big deal, as if he hadn't spent nearly a year avoiding the phone. "Hey, Bud, I thought it might be you."

He glanced at Marisala as he grabbed the towel that hung on the refrigerator-door handle. "It's Buddy Fisher," he told her.

Buddy Fisher. His agent. The man he'd worked so hard to avoid all these months.

"Great," Liam was saying into the telephone. "Eight months, okay. I'll try, and then . . . Yeah, I'll agree to that." There was a pause, and then he said, "Great, I'll talk to you tomorrow."

He hung up the phone and smiled at her. "Ready to go?"

They were meeting Santiago for Sunday brunch. Her uncle had flown up from San Salustiano upon hearing the news of her and Liam's engagement.

Marisala laughed. "Do you really think I'm going to let you leave this room before you tell me what that conversation was about?"

"Buddy Fisher called yesterday," Liam told her. "My publisher saw the column in the *Globe* and has offered me an eight-month extension on my book deadline. They've also offered to double my advance on the condition that if I *don't* write the book in eight months they can bring in their ghostwriter."

"Is that good?"

He laughed. "Yeah, I'd say so. Considering that I expected them to sue me for breach of contract."

"Do you think you can do it?" she asked seriously. "Spend all that time writing about what you went through?"

He held out his hand to her and she took it without hesitation. "I think I can try." He brought her fingers to his lips, kissing them lightly. "Come on. We don't want to make Santiago wait."

Marisala checked her hair in the entryway mirror. It was neatly combed, every curl in place. She wore one of her flower-print dresses, and she looked every bit the sweet young thing.

"You look beautiful," Liam said. He smiled. "Santiago will be pleased."

The Sunday newspaper was still sitting out in front of their condo door, and Marisala scooped it up. She would read her favorite columnist in the car on the way over to Santiago's hotel.

"Santiago will never know," Marisala told Liam as they started down the stairs to the lobby, "what lies beneath this dress."

"You're probably right," he agreed. He could smell the sweet fragrance of her freshly washed hair. "He won't realize that just because you look different, that doesn't mean you've changed."

"Well, yes," she said. "There's that. But what I was thinking is a little more literal." She gave him a decidedly wicked smile. "Santiago will never know that I am not wearing any underwear." Her smile got broader. "But *you* will."

Liam laughed. Dear God. He was going to sit there at brunch with Marisala and her uncle, his old friend, and he was going to be able to think of little else.

"I had to take steps to preserve my own identity," she explained. "This dress is not me."

"But going without underwear to Sunday brunch at the Ritz– that's you?"

"Absolutely."

"God, I love you."

Marisala smiled. "I know. I read it in the *Globe*."

THE EDITORS' CORNER

For some, March can be one of the coldest months of the season. But those with a heartwarming LOVESWEPT in hand know that it's easy to stay cozy during the harsh winter. This month we're going to take you from peaceful Tylerville, Indiana, to wild Hell, Texas. You'll have a chance to hear the roar of a stadium crowd . . . the irritated grunts of an injured inventor. LOVESWEPT once again covers the spectrum of readers' tastes with this month's batch of romance!

Mary Kay McComas returns with **MS. MILLER AND THE MIDAS MAN,** LOVESWEPT #874. Every time Augusta Miller looks out her kitchen window she sees a huge Rottweiler sitting on her garbage-strewn lawn. Next door, Scotty Hammond smiles each time the same sixteen cans come sailing back over his fence. His plan to meet his new neighbor is a bit unconventional, but Scotty is known all over town for getting things done one way or another. Now he's set his sights on Gus, and she's having no part of it! Can the single dad next door convince the lovely violinist to be his partner in life's duet? Mary Kay is at her best in this hilarious, yet touching story about kindred spirits who have much to learn about love.

Neither Annie Marsden, R.N., nor Link Sheffield, Ph.D., have a high regard for the opposite sex. To Annie, men are competitive macho studs; to Link, women are flighty and irresponsible. Now both are fated to **CHASE THE DREAM,** in LOVESWEPT #875 by Maris Soule. Injured in a lab explosion, a grouchy Link must wait out his recovery before he can get back to his work. Annie has taken care of rude patients before, and the pay for this job as Link's live-in nurse can't be beat. But when new dangers force them into hiding, Annie's job description is drastically altered. Can Annie keep the wary genius safe from the shadows that threaten both their lives? Maris Soule revels in the ultimate mystery of love in this tale of combustible passion and romance on the run.

How far would you be willing to go for a pair of tickets to the hottest game of the season? Domenic Corso and Lynne Stanford are willing to go **THE WHOLE NINE YARDS,** in LOVESWEPT #876 by newcomer Donna Valentino. As die-hard Steelers fans, Dom and Lynne realize their last, best hope of obtaining playoff tickets is to enter the special lottery and apply for a marriage license. The pair had hoped to keep their sweetheart deal a secret, until word of their pending, albeit pretend, nuptials reaches their friends and family! Will this harebrained scheme win them the tickets to the game, or will it succeed in sending them down the aisle for real? Please welcome Donna Valentino as she shows us what happens when a game of let's pretend gives way to something more real than ever imagined!

Hell, Texas. Population 892, that's including the barnyard animals. In Eve Gaddy's **AMAZING GRACE**, LOVESWEPT #877, Max Ridell learns that Hell really does exist. Although after being thrown in jail for defending himself against the town bully, Max is beginning to wish he'd never heard of the one-horse town and its sheriff, Grace O'Malley. Gracie admits that she's not one to stick out in a crowd, but Max makes her want, just once, to be the kind of woman a man could really fall for. Max has a few secrets to hide and Gracie's determined to find out just what's going on in her jurisdiction. Eve Gaddy's tantalizing novel delivers an undercover lawman into the arms of a tenderhearted sheriff and makes for a showdown not to be missed!

Happy reading!

With warmest wishes,

Susann Brailey *Joy Abella*

Susann Brailey   Joy Abella

Senior Editor   Administrative Editor

P.S. Watch for these Bantam women's fiction titles coming in February! *New York Times* bestselling author Amanda Quick once again stuns the world with

AFFAIR, now available in paperback. Private investigator Charlotte Arkendale doesn't know what to make of Baxter St. Ives, her new man-of-affairs. He claims to be a respectable gentleman, but something in his eyes proclaims otherwise. In **THE RESCUE,** by the versatile Suzanne Robinson, Primrose Adams disappears after witnessing a brutal murder on the streets of Victorian London. But when Sir Luke Hawthorne finds her, Primrose's secret pulls them together in a way neither can imagine. Hailed by *Romantic Times* as an author who "breathes life into an era long since past," Juliana Garnett returns with **THE VOW,** a dazzling medieval tale of intrigue and conquest. When William of Normandy sends his most trusted knight, Luc Louvat, to the northern reaches of Saxon England, Luc finds that it may be a lot more difficult to break down the defenses of a fair maiden than the fortress walls that surround her. And immediately following this page, preview the Bantam women's fiction titles on sale in January!

For current information on Bantam's women's fiction, visit our new Web site, *Isn't It Romantic,* at the following address:

http://www.bdd.com/romance

Don't miss these exciting novels
by your favorite Bantam authors!

On sale in January:

AND THEN YOU DIE . . .
by Iris Johansen

THE EMERALD SWAN
by Jane Feather

A ROSE IN WINTER
by Shana Abé

AND THEN YOU DIE . . .

by *New York Times* bestselling author Iris Johansen

Bess Grady is a hardworking photojournalist on an easy assignment. But what awaits her in a small-town paradise isn't pleasure; it's paralyzing fear. The unimaginable has happened in Tenajo—and Bess and her sister Emily have stumbled right into the middle of it. Suddenly, Emily disappears, Bess is taken captive, and escape seems impossible. But when rescue comes from an unexpected source, Bess is unprepared for the chilling truth. Tenajo was a testing ground—the first stage in a twisted game plan designed to spead terror and destruction. Now, to stop the ruthless conspirators whose next target may be the heartland of the United States, Bess must join forces with the intimidating stranger who led her out of Tenajo, a man whose motives are suspect, whose alliances are unclear, and whose methods have a way of leaving bodies in his wake. For she will do anything—risk everything—to save her sister, her family, and untold thousands of innocent lives.

"You slept well," Emily told Bess. "You look more rested."

"I'll be even more rested by the time we leave here." She met Emily's gaze. "I'm fine. So back off."

Emily smiled. "Eat your breakfast. Rico is already packing up the jeep."

"I'll go help him."

"It's going to be all right, isn't it? We're going to have a good time here."

"If you can keep yourself from—" Oh, what the hell. She wouldn't let this time be spoiled. "You bet. We're going to have a great time."

"And you're glad I came," Emily prompted.

"I'm glad you came."

Emily winked. "Gotcha."

Bess was still smiling as she reached the jeep.

"Ah, you're happy. You slept well?" Rico asked.

She nodded as she stowed her canvas camera case in the jeep. Her gaze went to the hills. "How long has it been since you've been in Tenajo?"

"Almost two years."

"That's a long time. Is your family still there?"

"Just my mother."

"Don't you miss her?"

"I talk to her on the phone every week." He frowned. "My brother and I are doing very well. We could give her a fine apartment in the city, but she would not come. She says it would not be home to her."

She had clearly struck a sore spot. "Evidently someone thinks Tenajo is a wonderful place or Condé Nast wouldn't have sent me."

"Maybe for those who don't have to live there. What does my mother have? Nothing. Not even a washing machine. The people live as they did fifty years ago." He violently slung the last bag into the jeep. "It is the priest's fault. Father Juan has convinced her the city is full of wickedness and greed and she should stay in Tenajo. Stupid old man. There's nothing wrong with having a few comforts."

He was hurting, Bess realized, and she didn't know what to say.

"Maybe I can persuade my mother to come back with me," Rico added.

"I hope so." The words sounded lame even to her. Great, Bess. She searched for some other way to help. "Would you like me to take her photograph? Maybe the two of you together?"

His face lit up. "That would be good. I've only a snapshot my brother took four years ago." He paused. "Maybe you could tell her how well I'm doing in Mexico City. How all the clients ask just for me?" He hurried on, "It would not be a lie. I'm very much in demand."

Her lips twitched. "I'm sure you are." She got into the jeep. "Particularly among the ladies."

He smiled boyishly. "Yes, the ladies are very kind to me. But it would be wiser not to mention that to my mother. She would not understand."

"I'll try to remember," she said solemnly.

"Ready?" Emily had walked to the jeep, and was now handing Rico the box containing the cooking implements. "Let's go. With any luck we'll be in Tenajo by two and I'll be swinging in a hammock by four. I can't wait. I'm sure it's paradise on earth."

Tenajo was not paradise.

It was just a town baking in the afternoon sun. From the hilltop overlooking the town Bess could see a picturesque fountain in the center of the wide cobblestone plaza bordered on three sides by adobe buildings. At the far end of the plaza was a small church.

"Pretty, isn't it?" Emily stood up in the jeep. "Where's the local inn, Rico?"

He pointed at a street off the main thoroughfare. "It's very small but clean."

Emily sighed blissfully. "My hammock is almost in view, Bess."

"I doubt if you could nap with all that caterwauling," Bess said dryly. "You didn't mention the coyotes, Rico. I don't think that—" She stiffened. Oh, God, no. Not coyotes.

Dogs.

She had heard that sound before.

Those were dogs howling. Dozens of dogs. And their mournful, wailing sound was coming from the streets below her.

Bess started to shake.

"What is it?" Emily asked. "What's wrong?"

"Nothing." It couldn't be. It was her imagination. How many times had she awakened in the middle of the night to the howling of those phantom dogs?

"Don't tell me nothing. Are you sick?" Emily demanded.

It wasn't her imagination.

"Danzar." She moistened her lips. "It's crazy but— We have to hurry. *Hurry*, Rico."

Rico stomped on the accelerator, and the jeep careened down the road toward the village.

They didn't see the first body until they were inside the town.

Let Jane Feather capture your heart once again with
the third and final book in her spectacular
"Charm Bracelet Trilogy"

THE EMERALD SWAN

by Jane Feather

Miranda, a gibbering Chip clinging to her neck,
dived into a narrow gap between two houses. It was so
small a space that, even as slight as she was, she had to
stand sideways, pressed between the two walls, barely
able to breathe. Judging by the cesspit stench, the
space was used as a dump for household garbage and
human waste and she found it easier to hold her
breath anyway.

Chip babbled in soft distress, his scrawny little
arms around her neck, his small body shivering with
fear. She stroked his head and neck even while silently
cursing his passion for small shiny objects. He hadn't
intended to steal the woman's comb, but no one had
given her a chance to explain. Chip, fascinated by the
silver glinting in the sunlight, had settled on the
woman's shoulder, sending her into a paroxysm of
panic. He'd tried to reassure her with his interested
chatter as he'd attempted to withdraw the comb from
her elaborate coiffure. He'd only wanted to examine
it more closely, but how to tell that to a hysterical
burgher's wife with prehensile fingers picking
through her hair as if searching for lice?

Miranda had rushed forward to take the monkey

away and immediately the excitable crowd had decided that she and the animal were in cahoots. Miranda, from a working lifetime's familiarity with the various moods of a crowd, had judged discretion to be the better part of valor in this case and had fled, letting loose the entire pack upon her heels.

The baying pack now hurtled in full cry past her hiding place. Chip shivered more violently and babbled his fear softly into her ear. "Shhh." She held him more tightly, waiting until the thudding feet had faded into the distance before sliding out of the narrow space.

"I doubt they'll give up so easily."

She looked up with a start of alarm and saw the gentleman from the quay walking toward her, his scarlet silk cloak billowing behind him. She hadn't paid much attention to his appearance earlier, having merely absorbed the richness of garments that marked him as a nobleman. Now she examined him with rather more care. The silver doublet, black and gold velvet britches, gold stockings and silk cloak indicated a gentleman of considerable substance, as did the rings on his fingers and the silver buckles on his shoes. He wore his black hair curled and cut close to his head and his face was unfashionably clean shaven.

Lazy brown eyes beneath hooded lids regarded her with a glint of amusement and he was smiling slightly, but Miranda couldn't decide whether he was smiling *at* her or *with* her. However, the smile allowed her to see that his mouth was wide and his teeth exceptionally strong and white.

Her own smile was somewhat uncertain. "We didn't steal anything, milord."

"No?" A slender arched black eyebrow lifted.

"No," she stated, flushing. "I am not a thief and

neither is Chip. He's just attracted to things that glitter and he doesn't see why he shouldn't take a closer look."

"Ah." Gareth nodded his understanding. "And I suppose some poor soul objected to the close examination of a monkey?"

Miranda grinned. "Yes, stupid woman. She screamed as if she was being boiled in oil. And the wretched comb was only paste anyway."

"That creature was on her head?" he asked, filled with compassion for the unknown hysteric.

"He's not a creature," Miranda protested. "He's perfectly clean and very good-natured. He wasn't going to hurt her."

"Perhaps the object of his attention didn't know that." The glint of amusement in his lazy regard grew brighter.

"That's always possible," Miranda conceded. "But I was about to take him away and they set on me, so what could I do but run?"

"Quite," he agreed, then cocked his head with a frown at the renewed sounds of a mob in full cry. "But I'm afraid they've realized you gave them the slip."

"Oh, lord of grace," Miranda muttered. "Come on, Chip." She turned to flee but the nobleman reached out and grabbed her arm.

"I have a better idea."

"What?" Miranda looked anxiously over her shoulder toward the sounds of the returning hue and cry.

"You'll be safer if you get off the streets for a while. That orange gown is as distinctive as a beacon. Come with me." He turned back toward the Adam and Eve without waiting for her assent and after an instant's hesitation Miranda followed him, Chip still clinging to her neck.

"Why would you bother with me, milord?" She skipped up beside him, her eyes curious as she looked up at him.

Gareth stared at her. The idea was far from fully formed, but the possibilities beckoned. "Would you be interested in a proposition?"

She looked up at him, and her blue eyes were wary. But she could see nothing in his countenance to alarm her. His brown eyes regarded her calmly, his mouth was relaxed. "A proposition? What kind of a proposition?"

A deeply enthralling, richly romantic novel of
passion and adventure by a stunning new voice in
historical romance . . .

A ROSE IN WINTER

by Shana Abé

*At sixteen, Lady Solange had pledged her love to Damon
Wolf, had dreamed they would be together forever. But
when her ruthless father threatened Damon's life unless
she agreed to marry another, Solange did the only thing
she could: she scorned her true love and sent him
away . . . never imagining the fate that awaited her,
never knowing that one day her destiny would be entwined
with Damon's once more.*

*For nine long years, Solange has lived a nightmare,
wed to a wealthy lord whose handsome face hides a soul of
darkest evil. Yet now, just as she is poised to finally make
good her escape, Damon suddenly appears at the castle gate.
Gone is the gentle hero of her childhood, replaced by a
fiercely attractive, thunderously angry knight, who makes
it clear he has never forgiven her betrayal. Convincing
Damon to escort her to safety will take all Solange's inge-
nuity—but the real challenge lies in breaching the walls
that Damon has built between them, to win back his
trust . . . and his hardened heart.*

    Solange.
    At last. It was a moment of epiphany. Here she
was in front of him, a grown woman, a widow by her
account. His mind was having a difficult time taking it
all in.

But his body was not, by heaven. He wanted her as fiercely as he ever did. He nearly could not breathe for the want.

He would not crumble, no matter the cost. He wanted to shout at her, he wanted to know why she had rejected him, why she had rejected her father, her homeland. Instead, he kept his lips tightly shut, marking her reaction to his news.

She turned away from him, took a few blind steps to the thronelike chair topping the dais. She did not sit, however, merely stood next to it, arms crossed over her chest. He saw the shiver take her again and again. Her head dipped low.

"My lady," he began.

"My father is dead. The earl is dead. I find—" Her voice broke, a tremulous waver before she recovered. "I find that I cannot think right now. I must rest."

As if on cue, the court women swarmed over to her, taking her arms and leading her down the steps. In frustration, Damon watched them go. He felt robbed of his moment after coming all this way. It couldn't be over this quickly. He would not allow her to disappear just yet.

"Countess," he called.

Solange stopped, then turned. The women fanned around her.

"I am weary," Damon said clearly. "I have traveled far to reach you. I require food and a place to bed for the night."

His words seemed to snap at her, drawing her spine straighter. "Of course. Forgive my poor manners. I'll have one of the men show you to your chambers and arrange to have dinner brought to you. I'm afraid it is past the evening meal, but there is always plenty of food in the buttery."

She murmured instructions to one of the ladies, who curtsied and fluttered away.

"Someone will be with you shortly," she said. "Good eve to you."

They left as a group out the chamber door, a flash of gold in a wash of pastels.

The fire popped and sizzled behind an iron grate, echoing off the emptiness around him.

He was awakened from a sound sleep by a hand placed over his mouth.

In an instant he had drawn the stiletto from beneath the pillow and pressed it against the throat of his attacker. It was a move so deeply ingrained from the years of battle that it took him a full minute to realize that both the hand and the throat belonged to a woman.

To Solange, to be exact.

The dimming fire allowed just enough of the delicacy of her features to stand out in the darkness. She showed no reaction to the sharp dagger but looked down at him calmly, waiting for the recognition to sink in.

He drew the knife back, then pushed her hand away. "Are you mad?"

"Shh. You must speak quietly, lest they hear you."

He tossed the covers off himself and climbed out of the bed. He was almost fully dressed, another habit learned from battle.

"What is the meaning of this, Countess? You have no place here."

"Please, Damon, lower your voice. They must not find us!"

He stared at her in the darkness, baffled. Her urgency was real enough; he reckoned if the newly widowed countess was discovered with another man on the very night of the death of her husband, her reputation would not survive.

The Solange he knew wouldn't have given a shrug of her shoulders over something like her reputation, Yet, she was the countess now.

"Leave," he ordered curtly.

She approached him slowly, hands held out in appeal. "It is my every intention to leave. That is why I'm here."

"What?"

"I want to go with you back to England. I want us to leave here tonight."

He laughed softly. "Your wits are addled, Solange. Go back to your women."

She made an exasperated sound. "The hounds of hell could not drag me back there. I have to go with you, tonight, right now."

She looked so thin and lovely, and very serious. A heavy black cloak swirled around her ankles, but as she moved toward him he saw to his amazement that she was wearing a tunic, hosiery, and buckskin boots: men's clothing. She was still talking.

"We need to leave as soon as you may be ready. I'll help you if you like." In the darkness she took on the earnestness of a young girl, breathless and beguiling. "I can pack very quickly."

He shook his head. "You'll not go anywhere with me, Countess. I'm not courting that kind of trouble. Seek your adventures elsewhere."

She paused, looking as if his barb might have actually hurt. He ignored the flash of guilt. She would not use him, damn her, for whatever game she was playing. He would not submit to that.

"You don't understand." Her voice was subdued. "I have to go."

"And why is that?"

She chewed on her lower lip, another girlish habit he found suddenly annoying. But then her face cleared, became resolute. "If you will not help me, then I will go alone." The cape billowed to life as she swept past him toward an opening in the far wall he had not noticed before.

He caught her before she could vanish into the blackness.

"What is this, madam? You have deliberately put me in a room with hidden doors and secret tunnels? Is it so that you may creep in here in the disguise of nightfall? Is that your amusement these days, Solange?"

"Of course. I knew you would bolt your door closed tonight. How else was I to get in?"

Her look was so innocent, he practically could believe in her virtue again. Amazing, this acting ability she had discovered.

How convenient for her to have a room to keep her lovers nearby, tucked away from prying eyes. What sort of husband had Redmond turned out to be, to allow his wife this unusual freedom in his own home? Damon was almost sorry he could not question him for himself.

"But the man is dead," he muttered. Very interesting.

"Pardon?"

"Your husband. I have just remembered myself. You are a widow driven mad with mourning, no doubt. Someone should be watching over you."

She shook him off with supple strength. "You have changed greatly, Marquess. You should not be surprised to learn that I have changed as well. You speak now of things you could not possibly know anything about. My apologies. I didn't mean to disturb you."

Before he could think to respond, she was gone, her footsteps fading away down the tunnel.

"Damn. Damn, damn, damn."

It was no accident, he knew, that she had chosen to throw back at him his own words from their parting those years past. She was too clever for it to be anything else.

She wasn't really fleeing the estate. She wouldn't act so rashly, he reassured himself. She had nowhere to go that he knew of. It would be a folly beyond belief to think she could make it back to England on her own—a woman, a gentlewoman, who really knew nothing of the ways of the world. She could not be that foolish.

With a muttered oath Damon picked up his scabbard and secured it around his waist. It took only a few minutes to toss his scant belongings back into the traveling sack, but he could feel each second slipping by.

He hurriedly shoved his boots on and laced up the sides. She would be at the stables by now, or who knew where that tunnel let her out of the house. She might have already had a horse waiting in some hidden location, in which case he would have to track her either by sound or wait until dawn, when he could see her horse's prints.

By dawn the entire household would realize their mistress was missing. And who would they first suspect in this dangerous mystery?

On sale in February:

AFFAIR
by Amanda Quick

YOU ONLY LOVE TWICE
by Elizabeth Thornton

THE RESCUE
by Suzanne Robinson

THE VOW
by Juliana Garnett

DON'T MISS THESE FABULOUS BANTAM WOMEN'S FICTION TITLES